THE DARKSIDE
OF SWEET

–For Those Who Had Faith In Me When I Did Not–

THE DARKSIDE OF SWEET

CHELLE FRESH

CONTENTS

CHAPTER 1: STORIES FOR RAINY DAYS

CHAPTER 2: DARK TALES

CHAPTER 3: AN EXCERPT FROM KIMBALL STREET

CHAPTER 1

STORIES FOR RAINY DAYS

So Many Men

I wouldn't say that I'm an ugly troll or tooth-shining Miss America, but my looks are fairly good for a forty something who has lived through it all. Here I am sitting on the couch trying to tell you a tale about why I wrote that first paragraph or why I call this little number, So Many Men.

Well, my sisters, and probably some brothers who secretly like reading romance novels; here it is in a nutshell. It all started a dozen years back when my husband Tyrone and I were divorcing. It was a very difficult time in my life as he was abusive and after seventeen years, I decided it was time to stop the violation of my life and the destruction of my world.

I remember how angry he was when the divorce became final; but underneath his anger, was hurt and despair. I almost felt sorry for him at that point; you see, I'm a sucker for the underdog and after he ranted for a few minutes, he wept like a newborn baby for what seemed like an eternity. My heart went out to him and I really wanted to cradle him in my arms, but the memories and a few aches from his previous abuses kept me from going near him and all I could do was walk away. I am a free woman again! Ha-ha!

When the movers came to take his things to his new place, my heart beat like African drums, the spirit of freedom pulsed within me like rivers overflowing their banks! It was a very momentous occasion; until, the door closed behind him and I heard the truck with him and his belongings pull off.

The silence in the room was deafening! I whistled in the air and I could swear I heard an echo of it bounce off the wall where his chair used be. Oddly enough though; even with my belongings still illuminating the place, it all seemed so barren. Suddenly, I was swept up in a swirl of loneliness pangs . . . God how I wished I had children! They would drive me crazy, but at least I'd have somebody to keep me company.

The loneliness lingered on for many moons after he left and I was sinking fast. I wanted male companionship something awful! I have to admit though, when Tyrone wasn't drunk, drugged or just plain in a rotten mood, he was very loving and tender. I miss those days when we would walk in the park and stay until the night was pitch black. We'd find ourselves lying on the ground looking up at the stars, making plans or talking about nothing. After an hour or so, we 'd make love like rabbits! Those were special times, believe it or not. Even though there were some beautiful moments buried underneath all the pain and suffering, I don't miss him exactly, but I've come to realize that I miss only the special times spent with a man.

Well now, I gotta tell ya; my prayers were answered when a new corporate manager was hired at the firm where I am employed as an executive secretary. All of the women, from executive to cleaning woman were dazzled by his electrifying smile and that great body in a tailored suit. I was too but I tried to maintain my composure as my suspicious nature took over my senses and snapped me back to reality. Sure, he's fine and cuts a dashing figure in a Yves Saint Laurent suit, but he could be Attila the Hun in disguise. So I kinda sorta decided all his "assets" were just window dressing and best for me to keep my distance. I admit I couldn't stay away from the temptation to look at him whenever he walked by my desk and it wasn't long before he made his rounds and had a need to see my boss, Mr. Barclay.

Moments later, Barclay called me into his office to introduce me to the mysterious man. Pleasantries were exchanged and when he flashed that mesmerizing smile, I felt warm and seemingly lost in some sort of spell. But all the while he must have felt the same way because we stood there staring into one another's eyes and shook hands for what seemed to be five minutes. The spell was broken by Old Man Barclay when he asked if we knew each other. We both snapped out of it and said no, but our glances said, "yeah baby, but we'd like to get to know each other wouldn't we?" Despite my better judgment and thinking he was some sort of monster, I was shocked to learn that I was in love! I went back to my desk humming and burning inside with a strange new sense of joy. I refreshed my makeup and fixed my hair better, hoping he'd stop by my desk before he returned to his office. I finished just in time as he came out of Barclay's office flashing that smile and window dressing for the ladies. He stopped by my desk and said, "Well Brenda, looks like we'll be working together from now on; I'm you're new boss." I nearly died from the extreme lust I had for the man! I recouped by asking in the most businesslike voice (or so I thought, but instead my voice came out sweet and dreamy). "What happened to Mr. Barclay?" Not that I really cared considering Old Man Barclay had been my boss for almost ten years and I never liked him. The feeling was mutual, he was a bigot in the biggest way possible! He hated the fact that he got a black woman to be his executive secretary and not only that, even if a white woman was to take my place he'd hate her too because you see, he didn't care too much for women period. Well anyway, Steven (that's his name) told me that Barclay was fired for embezzling funds from the company! I thought it was funny at first, then terror filled my soul as I might be implicated as a part of the crime. But Steven assured me that what Barclay did was strictly behind closed doors and after hours. So after we discussed Barclay and all the details of the files, Steven and I had lunch together at a executive members only club. It was quite swanky and I was in total awe! Every person there was worth millions! My only let down was that I was the only woman there, oops, my bad; let me rephrase that, the only black woman there. The food was delicious and quite expensive but since this was our first date, so to speak, I just ate daintily. We chatted and sipped wine for an hour beyond our scheduled lunch break. Hey, who am I to balk about being late? After all, he is the boss.

We exchanged information about ourselves and I found him to be a very interesting fellow. He is very well educated, speaks several languages and has traveled around the world twice. Or so what he led me to believe. Anyway, regardless of what lies he may or not be selling me, I was too dazzled by his charm. It seemed we were destined to be an item. But after a few days I discovered he was as cold as ice. What was on the outside did not match with his inside. I didn't want any bothering from him after I discovered that he really was a monster just as I had previously suspected. After I bid him goodbye, he refused to let me go. He kept saying that the relationship wasn't over until he said it was. It was then that I realized that this man was a spoiled, pampered soul and had never been denied anything within his relationships or in his life. Well baby, there is a first time for everything!

Our boss-employee relationship suffered as well as I should've known better to mix business with pleasure. But could you blame me? I was on a serious rebound and needed someone quick to fill the chasm of emptiness that Tyrone had left in my life. I came to the conclusion that Steven was no better than Tyrone despite his Yves Saint Laurent lifestyle; but at least for a few months, I wasn't lonely. However, Steven just wouldn't let it go and made my life a living hell on the job. I resigned and made damn sure that our path's would never cross again. Well, I was now lonely and jobless. But my employment situation picked up after I decided to try something other than secretarial work.

I took a job at a small but busy catering service and found that I enjoy this job deeply as the money was great as this company had clients up to the ying-yang! The tips were great too and the stress level I had experienced as an executive secretary was nonexistent. Who'd ever thought bussing and waiting tables could be so rewarding? The only down side to this job is that you are on your feet for many hours. I dealt with it though, but still, I had this void within me to fill. I wasn't interested in any of the guys that I worked with and too, I was wiser from my experience with Steven not to mix business with pleasure.

One night we catered a wedding party at a big meeting hall. I was serving a table when I saw this gorgeous hunk of man surrounded by many couples sharing light table banter. He looked so out of place sitting all alone at a couple's table, so I felt sorry for him and decided to speak to him as I refreshed his glass of champagne. His smile was electric and his voice was a deep Barry White baritone; I felt shivers play with my spine as he spoke. We briefly became acquainted and quickly exchanged telephone numbers as I had more people to serve.

Three days later after our chance meeting, he called me. His name is Jose and he is a surgeon at a teaching hospital. I was thrilled but I was disappointed when he told me that he had full blown Aids. It shocked me; but after he explained that he contracted it when an infected needle pierced through his glove during a surgery, I softened and put my fears away. He sincerely apologized for his frankness and told me he'd understand if I didn't want any bothering from him because of his affliction. But I admit, my first reaction was to run but then again, my affection for the underdog kicked in and I reassured him that I appreciated his honesty. We talked candidly about this situation and my fears as we talked as if we were old friends.

Two months later my relationship with Jose was going great! We did everything together and I was no longer empty. We were a couple for three years, which incidentally was longer than his doctor expected him to live. We spent many days in each other's company and tried to make each moment last forever. But at the end of the third year, his body was weakening and the changes in his health were rapid. On his good days, we'd go out on an outing and if he wasn't too exhausted, make love (protected of course) so passionate and erotic—well, you get the picture! He was the perfect man for me as he was everything I was searching for. Wasn't too long before we had fallen deeply in love, but it happened too late as after spending a wonderful Christmas with him at his vacation home in Vermont, he succumbed to his affliction in his sleep on New Year's day. One thing I am certain of though, he died a happy and cherished man. I'll never forget Jose as he gave me precious memories of what true love is.

Again a deeper void of loneliness enveloped me as I knew the odds of finding someone who'd love me like Jose were next to none. I grieved for many months and held on to the many happy memories with Jose. I tried not to be so bitter about the enemy that took him away from me. So in Jose's honor, I supported HIV/Aids research by participating in rallies, walk-a-thons and volunteered on an Aids hotline. That is where I met Carson. Tall, dark, muscular and sexy Carson! I could look at him all day! But after two months of friendship, I discovered he wasn't too sure of himself; as he didn't know whether or not he should come out of the closet. Unfortunately for me, a little after this confession, he had a sex change operation and now called himself Carla. Oddly enough we became the best of girlfriends and that friendship ended too because he, I mean, she met a wealthy business man and got married and moved to Brazil. It turns out that the love of Carla's life is Steven! I *really* wish them both well.

A year after Carson/Carla's departure, I decided to lay off men for awhile and I was going to be a free woman all the way. I went on single's trips and cruises, doing anything that pampered me and built up my self esteem. I met many men but kept them on the acquaintance level for the time being. They called every now and then wondering why I didn't want to get any closer to them. I explained that I was on the celibate circuit until I was ready for a more meaningful relationship. And so it went for 365 days and strangely enough, I wasn't lonely. I had eight good male friends who stopped by on occasion to take in a movie or go bowling or just to chat whenever theirs or my depression entered the scene. So many men but I didn't want any of them as lovers, and I reveled in the fact that just having them around was satisfying enough. Or so it seemed, until Roland, (#3 of 8) invited me to a New Year's Eve party.

Oh baby! Roland was looking soo fine and quite smooth in his tuxedo. Of course I was no slouch either in my slinkiest of the slinkiest black spaghetti strapped dress with matching drape. We were the best dressed couple at the party as all eyes were on us the whole time.

When the clock struck midnight and the New Year was wrung in, he surprised me by giving me the longest most passionate kiss I ever received since my relationship with Jose. I went limp and melted in his arms like butter! It just took my breath away and I was drowning in his spell. When he released me to come up for air, I was in a daze. He told me he had wanted to do that for a very long time and that he wanted to marry me. All I could say was "huh . . ." He thought I didn't believe him but I was still lost in that daze; he got on one knee and pulled out of his pocket a box that held the most stunning diamond engagement ring I'd ever seen. When my head cleared, my mind was saying no don't do it, you're not in love with him. But I must've been caught up in the moment as I felt my lips saying yes to his proposal. As the crowd graciously congratulated us and surrounded us with happy faces and clinking glasses of champagne, my mind kept saying to me, "why Brenda why?" And I told it, "I don't know."

Six months into our engagement, surprising enough I had fallen in love with him. I had seen a different side to him that as my friend I didn't notice. He was very loving and caring just as Jose was and I was beginning to think he was taken over by Jose's spirit. It was kind of frightening though as I thought I would never find anyone who could ever love me like Jose. There were many occasions where I was in doubt whether I was loving Roland because of who he was or was it that I was looking for another Jose. Many a moon I weighed the options and found that I liked Roland as Roland.

Another six months had passed and we were married. Everything was going delightfully smooth for the first two years of our marriage. We were happy in our two story home and there seemed that nothing could ever come between us. But I was wrong. I forgot about my mother-in-law.

The third year into my marriage to Roland, she started dropping by and spying. She was here everyday when I got home from work and worst yet, sometimes when neither of us were home, she'd be be standing outside waiting for one of us to let her in. That would be rain or shine believe it or not! I learned that she wasn't ready to let her baby boy go but why did she act like this now being that we were into our third year of marriage? Oh honey but things got worse when I got pregnant. It was suppose to be the happiest time of my life but Mommy Dearest, made me so uncomfortable, nervous and miserable that I miscarried. This hurt Roland deeply and had listened to his mother's accusations that I had lost the baby on purpose. That was the straw that broke this camel's back! I gave Roland an ultimatum, either he tells his mother to butt out or I was going to leave him. Shocks of all shocks, he told me to start packing.

Well, that was the quickest marriage and stupidest divorce ever written in the history books. Wish I knew about his Oedipus complex sooner, I wouldn't have married him knowing that Mother-in-law was part of the deal. I think I could've understood things better if I were competing with a woman on the side, a hooker or even playboy fold outs, but his Mother? Yuck!

Sigh, life goes on and once again I'm back in the lonely circle. I guess I was destined to be this way. Every time I think I got a good thing going on, something happens to take away the things that made it good. Maybe someday I'll hit the lottery and my good fortune will be my lover. But you know how that goes, you've got to play the game before you can win it and once you've won, a fool and his money are easily parted, or something like that. Hey what can I say? I'm no philosopher! I just know that love is game and it takes a lot of skill or luck to win it. So far I've won some and lost a lot!

Upon my fortieth birthday, I decided to go back on the celibate train. I realized that I don't have to always have a man in my life to enjoy it. Yes, it's nice to know that a man can bring some comfort and joy but there's always that fifty to fifty chance that he won't. I've been a witness to it all and have come to my senses to not let a man rule my life forever. I still have my health, my mind, my home and my looks. I also still have seven good male friends that will stand by my side when I need them. And again, I don't feel so lonely. I should've known better not to have gotten off this path when Roland proposed. If this situation ever arose again, this time I will listen to my mind and follow it's advice without question. Sorry heart, but you don't always know what's best. There are more stories like this that played and replayed in my life; but I don't think you want to hear about it. That would make my story repetitious and may bore you enough to cause fountains of tears. So my friends, this has been my tale and I gotta go now. I've got a date with the man upstairs; no my darlings, It's not what you think, I mean God. I'm on my way to church. I've found another way to channel my energies as I feel better knowing that there is no such thing as loneliness when you put your life in God's hands. Maybe someday I will find Mister right, but what will be, will be if it is God's will. But in the meantime I am happy to serve the Lord as I hear good things come to those who wait on Him; so far this is true as I've found a true and greater love without having the troubles of being in the arms of so many men.

IN YOUR ABSENCE

"Push Nikki push! You can do it . . . PUSH!!" said Nathan trying to encourage her. "I . . . I AM dammit!!!!! I . . . I'm pushing as hard as I can . . . just make it stop!!!" Screeched Nikki as the pain and stress of the birth increased in its intensity. The pain was so great that she held Nathan's hand so tight that he was beginning to lose the circulation in it. Nikki's obstetrician and his nurse worked furiously at their end trying to bring a new life into the world. Dr. Magen replied, "Just a little more Nikki, I see the crown of the head . . . ." "I can't . . . I'm so . . . so . . . tired . . ." "You can do it Nik . . . come on sweetie, just one more big one . . . on the count of three, ok? One, breathe in Nik . . . Two, that's it . . . you're doing fine . . . Now exhale . . . Three! Push hard Nikki!!!" Nikki bared down and pushed as hard as she could as she wanted this baby out of her asap.

Nathan tried his best to comfort her as much as possible but he was out of his element when it came to stuff like this. He is a single man with no wife or girlfriend nor had he ever conceived a child with anyone. His whole life centered around the coldness of the business world and this was completely new to him. For the first time in his life he was scared and yet filled with such wonderment. He didn't know why he was so fascinated about this as he wasn't the father of the baby nor did they have such a relationship as he was her husband's best friend and her boss. But something inside him made him proud as if he were the father and had made love to her. He always enjoyed being in her company as they worked closely together at the office and was always lending a hand as a friend to Nikki and her husband, who incidentally decided after the announcement of her pregnancy, to disappear into thin air.

Dr. Magen said quite excitedly, "Ok Nik, the shoulders are out, keep pushing dear, that's it . . . a little more!!" Nathan rubbed her back and kept wiping the sweat off her brow and her tears from her face as she strained to push the baby completely out. Finally she screamed loudly as she felt the force of the baby passing out of her and two seconds later another slipped through effortlessly. "Oh my goodness! I don't believe it! There's two of 'em!" said Doc Magen as he worked to free them from the goos and matter that surrounded them and gave each baby a little tap on the rump to make it breathe. Nathan hugged Nikki as they each wept tears of joy and relief. "Mr. and Mrs. Peterson, you are the proud parents of identical twin boys!" Doc Magen said gleefully as he and the nurse worked to cut the cord and clean the babies off. Nathan and Nikki were so overcome with joy that they didn't hear what the doctor called them. They beamed at one another as the babies continued to wail after they were cleaned, wrapped in blankets and presented to them. Nathan kissed Nikki on the forehead, "you done good kid . . ." She replied with extreme tiredness in her voice, "you weren't so bad yourself, boss . . . without your coaching, I don't think I . . . oo . . . what the? . . . OWWW . . . !!" "What's wrong Nik? What's happening?!?" asked Nathan. The nurse took the babies and put them in layettes and took them to the nursery while Doctor Magen checked Nikki out to find out what caused her pain. "Nikki, I want you to push hard again . . . you may have another arrival on its way." Said Doctor Magen. "What? You can't be serious!" exclaimed Nathan. Nikki replied tiredly, "Oh no . . . you've got to be kidding!" Doc Magen was very perplexed by this as the ultrasound only showed one fetus not three nor did the second or third child's heartbeat appear on any of the heart monitor's scans. This was very perplexing indeed. Nikki was overly exhausted now after virtually completing 24 hours of the birthing process, and to everyone's amazement there was a third. But after all their efforts, unfortunately and sadly, it was stillborn.

As Nikki was being transported from the recovery room, Nathan walked along side the gurney that carried his friend and secret love to her room. The attendants locked the bed in place and made sure she was comfortable; they left and Nathan sat in the chair by her bedside and held her hand as he quietly prayed. Being a very Christian man, he was grateful to God to have allowed him to witness the miracle of birth as he had no one in his life to fill that capacity for him. He had been living his goal/fantasy of being a husband and a now presently, a father through Nikki and Leon's lives. He thanked the Lord for this gift and prayed for Nikki and her babies. His meditation was soon interrupted as Doctor Magen came in to talk to the father of the children. "Mr. Peterson, I have some papers for you to sign, and have you and your wife discussed names for the babies yet?" Nathan smiled and replied, "Doctor Magen, I'm Nathan MacMillian, I'm not the children's father nor is Nikki my wife, I was here just to offer my support." "Oh I beg your pardon, then sir, are you a relative?"

"No, I'm just a friend of the family. We have no idea where Mr. Peterson is at this point." Nathan felt a sadness fill him as he revealed this to Doc Magen. It was such a cold thing for Leon to do at a time like this. The Petersons had been separated for a year before she became pregnant with Leon's children; but despite the separation, she allowed Leon to come home on occasion with the sincerest hope that they could patch things up. Things looked positive until she became pregnant. Nathan recalled how excited she was when she called him from the doctor's office about the outcome of the tests. Being that this was her first pregnancy, she was so sure that this event would bring her and Leon closer together as a family. But as soon as Leon was told, he decided then and there it was time to vanish off the face of the Earth. This broke Nikki's heart and she became very despondent. Nathan was concerned for her welfare and health; after all, he was a friend and knew she needed a helping hand, but, he didn't expect to fall in love with her. Nathan was very deep in thought over this and had blocked out most of the good doctor's conversation.

Suddenly a strange feeling washed over him and he interrupted the doctor. "Hey Doc? Is it possible that I could sign the birth certificate as their father, you know like a legal guardian?" "Well young man, being a legal guardian is a big responsibility. Yes, you can sign but you'll have to get Nikki's consent first." "Don't think that'll be a problem Doc, how soon will you need this information?"

"It can wait til tomorrow, let her sleep, she's had a rough night. So, are you planning to adopt her children?" said Doc Magen with a fatherly twinkle in his eye. Nathan glanced at Nikki while she slept deeply and replied before the good doctor left, "Yes, I am." His heart beat wildly at the idea and couldn't wait to tell her. He beamed with pride as again, he had something joyous to pray for, and had hoped that his dream of having a family would finally come true.

FIFTEEN YEARS LATER

Nathan, Nikki and the twins, (named Nathan Jr. and Nicholas after their parents respectively) lived together happily as a family. It was on the twins' fifteenth birthday that Nathan and Nikki revealed the truth about themselves and their natural father. Nathan and Nikki didn't know what to expect but the twins surprised them by making it known that Nathan was the only father they had ever known and as far as Leon was concerned, he never existed nor would they accept him as their father. They prayed as a family for Leon afterwards and continued being one happy family.

TIME PASSES

The twins grew to become fine Christian men. Nathan Jr. aspired to be a writer and went away to college to fulfill his dream. Nicholas on the other hand was still unsure what he aspired to be, but he wanted to travel and joined the Air Force to make his mark on the world. Regardless of what direction the boys took, Nikki and Nathan were very supportive and before the boys left for their individual destinies, it was decided that it was time for Nathan and Nikki to finally marry.

WEDDING DAY

Everything was going so well for Nikki and Nathan until the pastor got to the part of where he says: "Is there anyone here with any moral reason to object to the joining of these two people, speak now or forever hold your piece." Out of nowhere, a male voice objected and the church was stunned. Barreling down the aisle came a familiar face; an angry, stormy person readying for a fight. People in the pews began to whisper and gossip; for those who knew this angry figure, thought he was dead and for those who did not know, his entrance just ruined the most romantic wedding they ever witnessed. Shock was on every face as he approached Nikki, Nathan and the wedding party. He said as he glared at their faces of shock, "I object to this! Damn right I do!! She's still my wife dammit and he stole her away from me! She never divorced me and I want her back!!" He went to grab for her but Nathan stepped to him to protect Nikki and said for all to hear, "Church, this is not true. Yes, they were separated. And during that time she was still deeply in love with him; so deep was that love that she tried to make her marriage right again and never even looked at me in any other way other than a brother and her boss. But as soon as she became pregnant with his children, this man who stands before you ran out and disappeared.

Through the years of my friendship with him, I observed that he never really loved her and after all this time, now wants to "stake his claim." I, Nathan S. MacMillian have been by her side, doing the things he should've done. I didn't steal her away as Leon suggests; I sought the advice and guidance of the Lord even before entering this relationship and it was He who granted His blessings for Nikki and I to be together. In his absence, I have been husband, father, lover and friend; where was he when the twins were being brought in this world? Where was he when they said their first words, took their first steps or graduating from high school? Should he be allowed to come in here and stake his claim to a life he threw away years ago? I say, no. We are within our legal rights to marry according to law and in the eyes of the Lord." Leon rolled his eyes as he thought, "Oh brother, *when* will he ever get off his soapbox? Always making speeches, it's a wonder we were friends all these years!" Then Nathan turned to Leon and said, "You were my best friend and I even considered you as a brother. You should be standing here as my best man, but brother, those times have passed; we forgive you and you may stay to be a witness but you cannot claim what no longer belongs to you."

The church applauded his speech and Leon was silent for a long time. He looked upon the faces in the pews and saw something he didn't expect; they really had forgiven him! Then he looked in Nikki's eyes and saw the love that she had for him now belonged to Nathan, his best friend since childhood. He took her hand in his and kissed it and gave her his blessing to wed. She gave him a hug and thanked him then she introduced him to his sons. He smiled with pride and envy as they stood by their surrogate father's side readying to back him up if any rough stuff occurred. They were tall, strong and handsome and he had to admit to himself that Nathan and Nikki had done an excellent job in raising them. He felt ashamed too as despite his running out on them, he knew he couldn't be the father or man Nathan was. But the truth was he never gave himself a chance either, but still was glad in knowing that he was forgiven and that they gave him a chance to finally do the right thing. He apologized to everyone and started to make his way up the left side aisle of the church to leave, but the twins ran after him and stopped him; they hugged him and then seated him in the front row. The wedding proceeded and everything was right with the world again.

HIGH DRAMA

A short play written by Chelle Fresh

Narrator:	*As a bright sunny afternoon cascades over the business sector of downtown anywhere USA, the hustle and bustle is halted on the main street as a jumper stands on a ledge of the 10th floor of a newly constructed office complex. The crowd below is held captive by the sight; anticipation grows thick and then some wiseass begins to chant: "JUMP! JUMP!" Like a disease it spreads and the crowd is now in a frenzy with eager hope the jumper will do just that. Meanwhile, up on the ledge a very pregnant young lady stands on her perch and shouts back at the crowd below.*
Jumper:	"Go away you bloodthirsty bastards! Let me jump in peace!"
Wise Ass:	"Why don't you stop talking and jump already! I only got an hour for lunch ya know!"
Crowd:	Me too! (*Laughter*)
Jumper:	"Kiss my ass! I'll jump when I'm good and ready!!"
Angry Lady:	"Oh no she didn't! I know she ain't talkin' to me! I'll come up there and push her off my damn self!"

Narrator:	*Many people in the crowd agreed with the lady and made similar comments. At this point, the onlooking crowd had become an ugly mob scene. The police now had their hands full as fights broke out amongst the crowd as everyone began to push and shove to get near the entrance of the building so they could get at the jumper. Meanwhile the jumper laughed at them as she watched the silliness unfold on the ground. Police were everywhere and they seemed to have forgotten her. Then as she gazed out over the horizon, the landscape of the city all of a sudden became beautiful in her sight. She as so lost in the picturesque view that she hadn't noticed a handsome young priest coming out onto the ledge. A few policemen were at the window trying to keep the crowd on the inside from getting too close and also causing a scene.*
Priest:	"Hello, uh miss . . . ."
Jumper:	*(Startled almost slipping off ledge. But the Priest catches her in the nick of time)* "Arrgggh!! Don't do that! You almost made me fall!!"
Priest:	"Well, isn't that what you want to do?"
Jumper:	"Yeah, but when I'm ready to do it! But not one minute sooner okay?"
Priest:	"May I ask why you want to destroy yourself and your baby?"
Jumper:	*(She chuckled to herself)* "Do you really want to hear this?"
Priest:	"Certainly my dear, its what I do best."
Jumper:	"Well, it's a long story Padre. My life went from perfect to zip just like this" (snapping her fingers, then Jumper breaks into Rap, "High Drama")

"Give me a reason to live, I just got married and a bought a house, everything was fine and quiet as a mouse. One month later to my dismay, a little one was on its way. Mother-in-law got evicted, now my space is restricted. Tension is bad for your Karma, I wish I could escape this "HIGH DRAMA!""

Give me a reason to live, I went outside, it started snow, the temperature dropped to four below, I stayed too long and got frostbitten, came in the house while the cat was having kittens! Lost my job, I began to sob, as I lost my husband to a man named Bob! Give me a reason to live, my life reeks, I gave up hope, so here I stand at the end my rope. Mother-In-Law got evicted now my space is restricted. Tension is bad for your Karma, wish I could escape this Hell called "High Drama!!""

Priest: "I see your point, but it's not worth killing yourself over. There are other options, bet you haven't given them any thought have you?"

Jumper: "Look, I've had it, Okay? My life is over!"

Priest: "Everybody goes through bad times sometimes sweetie. You have to learn that bad times are just little tests of faith. So if you jump off this ledge what will this act prove?"

Jumper: "It'll prove a lot of things that's what. I'll prove that no one cares. Look at them down there, they came to see a show, they want me to jump. I'll even bet my homo husband is sitting somewhere with his lover having a good laugh about this.

Priest: "Have you talked this over with your husband or anybody? Am I the only person you've told this to?"

Jumper: "Yes, you're the first person I told. Nobody seemed to care, so I didn't even bother to say anything."

Priest: "How about you come inside with me so we can discuss those options I mentioned. I promise I won't be real preachy but I guarantee that the solutions I will offer will clear your mind and your soul of all the troubles that surround you. But you have to trust me before we begin the healing process. Take my hand and come inside with me."

Narrator: *The Priest held out his hand to lead her off the ledge and inside the safety of the building. The Jumper was silent for a long while but she studied his face and felt a calmness fill her. Something about him let her know that what she was doing was wrong. And that if no one else in this world cared, this man really did. She looked down at the angry mob below that was still calling for her demise and then she looked at the Priest. She grabbed his hand and decided not to give the assholes below the satisfaction of seeing her body splattered on the pavement and see her make the biggest mistake of her life. The police officers on the inside assisted the Priest 's efforts to bring the Jumper in. Once inside, the officers kept the onlookers away from them as he led her into a conference room away from the prying eyes of the small crowd that also had grown inside and they began to chat.*

Priest: "Even though I said I wouldn't get too preachy but I must tell you that God cares. Cause you see if He truly didn't care He wouldn't have sent me out there to stop you. God is the first option for your healing. Do you go to church?"

Jumper:	"No, but I used to before I got married. I don't know why I stopped."
Priest:	"It happens. But you need to go back. Speak with your pastor and ask for counseling. He can help you get help for your mother-in-law and for you and your baby. It's like the song says, Where is your faith in God. *(Sings, "Where Is Your Faith In God")* "Faith, is the substance of things afar. The evidence of things we can't see . . . . Faith, faith, where is your faith, in God? Oh, oh, faith will move mountains, oh faith will open the fountain, oh faith will help you succeed, oh faith will supply your every need oh where is your faith in God?"
Cop:	"Oh yeah!"
Cop and Priest:	"Where is your faith in God!?!"
Priest:	"If you have a faith, you have the solution to any problem that arises. If you had jumped, the only thing your death would prove was that you had no faith that God will deliver you from the bad times. Plus, I want you to think about the baby that you are carrying, did it deserve to be punished for something it had no control over? Faith is your key to success young lady. Go back to church and you'll see things in a better perspective, I guarantee it."
Jumper:	"You're right Padre, I had let my faith slide. I'll take your advice and get help right away."
Priest:	"Good. Glad to hear it."
Narrator:	*Just then the Priest's beeper goes off.*

Priest:	"Excuse me I've got to run. But remember what I told you, faith is the key to everything. Good luck young lady and God Bless."
Narrator:	*The Priest shook her hand goodbye and went on his way. The policemen that stayed with them escorted her out of the building by going out of a side entrance away from the mob inside and outside of the building. As she walked downtown feeling uplifted and filled with a new sense of joy, she decided to buy a newspaper and to treat herself to lunch at a nearby cafe. After being seated and her meal ordered, she decided to read the newspaper while she waited for it to be served. When she got to the obituary page, her face went white. A picture of a man who had jumped off a ledge of his office building a few days ago was being funeralized today. His name was Zachary Nemez and he worked at the building where she was about to jump from. She almost couldn't catch her breath because Zachary Nemez was an insurance broker but yet he came to her rescue disguised as a priest. After eating her meal, she went to Zachary's viewing.*
Old lady:	"Excuse me, Miss? Are you a related to us in any way? I don't recall seeing your face at any of the family reunions."
Jumper:	"No, not related. I used to be a client of Mr. Nemez's. Just came to pay my respects."
Narrator:	*The old lady went over to the family members and friends and told them that she was a client of Zachary's. This satisfied their curiosity and allowed Jumper to meditate in peace. Soon she was alone in room.*

Jumper: *(She spoke softly as she stood by the casket)*
"Mr. Nemez I came here to thank you for what you did today, I promise you sir, I will regain my faith and live life to its fullest; no more high dramas for me. God Bless you Mr. Nemez."

The End.

A LADY IN WAITING

Dear Mr. 2b:

If you are pondering, wondering, questioning, guessing, seeking, waiting, contemplating for the right time to know me then may I offer that you let this manner of expression explain.

I want a man who can take me out for the evening and make it special although there is no reason to be other than enjoying each other's company. I want to walk under moonlit skies sharing a kiss, a bottle of wine and memorable moments with you.

I want a man who can take me in his arms, kiss me ever so passionately as much as possible and stoke a fire where there is nothing but old cinders and fond remembrances. To take me to that point of no return quietly, then sweetly drift to caress, cuddle and be spoken to tenderly afterward and maybe just maybe, do it all over again.

I want a man to be encouraging when my aspirations need a boost. To be strong when the hazards of the day befall me and I need comforting to make it through.

I want a man who can be Mr. Fixit as well as Mr. Mom in a pinch. One who will be able to weather my emotional storm when I am vulnerable and play Doctor when I am sick.

Are you the man who can return all my affections with the same passion and ultimately much more to keep me happy and satisfied? One with the stamina to keep up with my moments of hyperactivity and can make me feel safe on all scopes of my plane? If this is you, then ponder, wonder, guess and contemplate no further as meeting you is my aim.

What Jiminy Cricket Sez

High fiddle dee dee
An actor's life for me
Jiminy Cricket once said.
But when he opened his mouth to act, they threw him out on
his head.

From place to place and stage to stage he quoted that same ol'
monologue; until one day,
he realized it was better to find a steadier job!

So now, Jiminy Cricket sez
High fiddle dee dee Acting's not for me; so now I collect pay, for
making the actors day. I'm an agent now you see, if you want
fame then honey you got to pay me.

LOVE'S REFRAIN

A secretary is at her desk typing countless memos and other correspondence when the phone rings, she picks it up and offers the standard business salutation. She smiles at the familiar voice of her husband, who at this point is at his desk shuffling the same amount of papers. "Let's meet after work in Rittenhouse Square, under your favorite tree; we'll have dinner and take in a movie afterwards." He said lovingly. She agreed and they finished their chat. After a few minutes of basking in the glow of their plans, she was brought back to reality when she saw the stack of papers, and at her husband's office, he too came to the same realization.

The work day had come to an end and she gave a sigh of relief as she left the building. She did not want to see another piece of paper as long as she lived, or at least not until tomorrow. She walked to the park and when she arrived at their meeting place, she sat down on the bench and waited for her husband.

She looked at the tree and touched her initials that were carved into the tree by a faded childhood love that still lurked deep in her heart. She touched his initials and felt a warm feeling fill her soul. She closed her eyes and thought of him. Suddenly, she was startled by a familiar voice; it was him! Was this a dream? Was this really happening? They hugged and talked about their past, but before they could get deeper into their conversation, a female voice called him and her husband called to her. They shook hands and said their goodbyes and understood the secret messages their eyes expressed for one another.

Her husband asked suspiciously, "who the hell was that?"

She simply replied, "Oh just someone I knew a longtime ago."

"Enough said." he quipped, catching the strange gleam in her eyes. Her husband took it calmly as he was secure in knowing that his wife was faithful and would never cheat on him; and so he never gave this incident another thought. However, on the other side of the coin, her childhood flame's companion was not so understanding nor forgiving.

Life As A Flea

(A Short Monologue and a disgusting life!)

Hi! I'm a flea and I suck blood from most forms of life and I'm
very seldom seen; I'm real real tiny but I'm totally mean!
I hop from dogs, I pounce on cats but really prefer human blood
opposed to a rat's!

Some of the ways people try to exterminate us fleas is really
really dumb! Don't you know that escaping assassination is a
fleas' rule of thumb?

I'm not a vampire, I'm not a leech; just a itty bitty biting itch
making little pest.
And if I had to compare my life to yours,
I'd say life as a flea is the best!

A Good Man
Is Hard To Find

I need no man to take care of me, I can take care of myself in every way and of course financially.

I need a doctor when it comes to curing my ills, but Hell if I'm going to lay with him just to pay my overdue bills.

I may need a lawyer when it comes to a legal matter ending in a courtroom fight, but in my house especially in my bedroom, I am in control because I know my legal rights.

I need no man's protection from anything, I can fend and protect myself; but who's going to protect him from me when his machoism overflows and he can't seem to help himself.

I don't need a man to do anything but love me, that's all I'll ever need one for because nothing nor nobody will keep me from my goals to strive ahead.

But when it comes to that never ending search for Mr. Right, a good man is hard to find and it gives you that sinking feeling that the good ones are either married, gay or dead!

A Fantasy Begins

As he sat intensely at his computer terminal, she entered the room with her usual exuberance; cheerful and bouncing with life. He looks up from the terminal, offers a weary smile and a hello. She sits in a chair that is behind him as he returned to his difficult task. Moments pass and she interrupts him with a stupid but brief question: "Are you busy?" He makes an error and snaps at her, "yes isn't obvious that I am?" He rubbed his tired eyes and cradled his aching head in his hands.

She, understanding her interruption was costly, begins to massage the tense muscles of his neck and shoulders. He relaxes a little, but stops her and stands before her. He says, "thanks for your help but I've got a ton of work to do. Don't you have something better to . . . do;" he looked into her eyes realizing the true concern she has for him. She smiles and he smiles too; they gaze into one another's eyes and kiss passionately. Response led to response and before they realized it a love was consummated that was always only in his dreams.

Suddenly, there was a knock at the door—scramble! A rude awakening as he realizes it was nothing but a dream. Wiping the sleep from his eyes, he glanced at his screen and sees the same error that was on it in his dream. Still, there was knocking at the door; he yelled, "come in, its open!" His eyes are now open wide with surprise as she entered with her usual exuberance. But she stopped in her tracks when she saw the strange look on his face. She said with deep concern, "something the matter? Looks as if you've seen a ghost."

He replied, still in shock, "no, no . . . I uh fell asleep at my computer . . . just have to shake loose the cobwebs that's all." Still a little hesitant, she replied, "if you're still sleepy or busy I can come back some other time." He says, "no not at all, by all means come in. Have a seat, actually I'm glad you stopped by . . ."

And so it begins.

WORK

Sitting here at the main desk, hoping that the phone doesn't ring, waiting for the end time, waiting for the clock to speed up and work to dissolve, tensions released and I can finally go home.

Sitting here in the main office not knowing what really to do as its hard to learn all the procedures especially when you work some place else and these operations don't apply to you.

Sitting at the main desk, shit!, the phone just rang and I don't know what to say. Just waiting for the end time listening to the time clock slowly tick away. Work is beginning to dissolve, tensions are released and I want to go home.

Sitting here at the main desk, now it is the end time, listening to the clock telling me its tick tock rhyme; tensions dissolved, work released, its that time and I can finally go home.

The Bad, Bad, Bad Hair Day

Momma always said there'd be days like this!

Oh boy! What a mess! How many of you out there have gone to the hairdressers or beauty shop, spending countless hours and dollars on that special haircut or style to make you feel gorgeous and en vogue, only to have it taken away in the matter of minutes by the forces of nature? Well, I for one am a victim of those forces as Mother Nature has taken an extreme dislike for me and wants to derail my self esteem. Think of the money, the time and effort of the stylist and time spent under dryers!

Hours of getting the hair primed and primped just so, then the moment you step outside, WHOOSH! POOF! SPLATT! After taking a beating from wind, rain and humidity our friend hair, does a sad, slow but overly dramatic FLOP in our faces. Sad but true! It's enough to make a grown person cry! I know I do cause when someone sees me after one of these incidents I tire of hearing, "you paid for that style? I thought you got your hair done, what happened?" ARGHH!! Enough already! My solution to it all is wear a wig! But be careful that Mother Nature doesn't whip up a hurricane or an extreme wind tunnel just because you're wearing a wig. It's funny how she always knows when to do these things; its like Mother Nature has radar or ESP or something. *Beep, beep, beep* Wig wearer at 10:00; send in a whirlwind stat! Ut-oh, freshly done hair, send rain now!

Well, whatever her reasoning for torturing people who have hair, people who are follicle challenged should think of how lucky you are not to have Mother Nature as your personal torturer! Rejoice bald folk, dear Mother Nature can't harm what you don't have! That is why I am getting shorn the next go around. So go ahead Mom Nature,do your worse now cause when my hair is too short for you to muss, you are going to feel quite salty! Go pick on somebody else for a change, I'm tired of being your favorite victim and tired of having bad hair days.

Enuff said.

A Strong Woman's Blues

What a life! Sheppard is back in my life and I'm not so sure of his intentions. He's definitely a carouser; a coke head and alcoholic, and big time skirt chaser. I don't usually associate with men like that . . . but I don't know why I am so attracted to him. Maybe I'm just too needy right now. My husband A. J. and I have been separated eight months now and during this time I really hadn't met anyone new. Not one nibble so to speak. Then all of a sudden, like roaches coming out of the woodwork, men were visible.

My friend who is now my boss, Marlon, has been calling constantly but it's all business with him. It would be nice if we could be alot more friendlier. He acts as if he is afraid to be with me. I don't want to marry him, nor do I want sex from him either. I want the type of relationship Jason Courtland and I had a few years back. Some affection, companionship and fun. Sure we were sometimes sexual, but it wasn't the old formula. There was passion and discovery, a wonderment to it. He liked hugging and putting his arms around me and I liked it too. I'm not asking for a deep commitment, just a little care. Sheppard gave me twenty dollars yesterday and it freaked me out; outside of A. J. owing me child support and the times when we were courting, no man ever really gave me anything! They just took from me. The only thing given was sex; which in itself is a give and take anyway. Men take it and a needy person like myself gives it. And in return, they get what they want and I still come up empty. Nothing to show that I'm in a relationship or at least they cared about me sincerely. I envy people like my sister and her friend Jilly; because they are the total embodiment of what men like in a woman; their hair is just so, their bodies are curvy and they are so damned cutesy without putting on an act and they get what they want from men without batting an eyelash. They may not do anything that is outlandishly "girlish", but they are real women. God I wish I was like that! I saw my problem coming while I was growing up. The male species always overlooked me. They liked being around me but they wouldn't get close. I can be the best pitcher in a baseball game, top scorer in a basketball game but the sex game, hah, I wouldn't be even be considered. I'm discovering at this age, that I am too "male" for my own good. I should've taken my cues from my teen days when I liked Stevie B. Back in the days when we were too young to know what sex was or what it entailed; those innocent days when the boys chased the girls and when they caught us the makeshift "courting ritual" would begin, but not for me! When they chased me I continued to run until they gave up! I remember the only one who'd chase me continuously was Wilson Gregory Stroud, to me, back then he was just some disgusting boy! He was three years older and I at thirteen hadn't fully matured mentally in the flowering that woman go through. But if he ever came back into my life today, I would welcome him with open arms, that is, if he'll have me. I've flowered alot but basically, I'm still the old me and it was a tough time in my life; femininity is something that according to my mother, is instinctual; but for me that instinct is just kicking in now that I'm getting really close to forty! I wish I could go back and change the way I treated ol' "Stinky" Stroud; I think he really liked me for me; not because I was sexy, nor very girlish, but he liked me because he knew I was a strong woman who could best any male almost at anything and wouldn't cry over the smallest of hardships. I think he liked the competition between his strong athletic, intelligent Adam and my strong athletic, intelligent and talented Eve; I was a challenge and he wanted to win. But I was too clever and quick; using talent and skill over those womanly wiles that everybody else was using to get what they want. I was hoping my talents would carry me through but I realize now the importance of femininity. It's a lonely road being too strong, too talented and too damn intelligent. But I must say thank you to Stroud, because as I look back at my life, he was the only one who saw in me all the femininity in the world while everyone else was too busy running away and giving up on me as a candidate for womanhood and its games that males and females must play.

When my eyes opened a little in the femininity department and I dated, I always wondered why the guys never treated me like other girls. You know, getting showered with gifts, given money for the upkeep of appearance, taken places you know the guy can't afford and being shown off. I am just as good looking as anybody else and in some instances look better than most. All I get for my troubles is a cheap or free date, or they'd come over and just sit in front of my TV like it was God. Then it was time to get what they want; this discouraged me alot-why was I treated so differently? I gave up to the ones I really wanted to give it up to-but I gained nothing in return. There it is again-that give and take syndrome. They took + I gave=nothing in it for me. Just pure sexual satisfaction for him and very infrequent for me. But on the material plane I am used and thrown away like a dust rag. Some men make damned sure that the woman they have continue to look good and make sure their financial needs are met to keep them happy, "to keep" them so to speak; they pay for hairdressers, nail salons and clothes, the woman may not have enough money to pay for toilet paper and her "man" would come to the rescue. But not for me!?! I pay the mortgage, electric, gas, telephone, water bill and child care and toilet paper needs, I work hard and in return for all those things mentioned above, hair dressers, nail salons and the like are luxuries I deny because I can't afford them.

Even though I was married to A.J. for fifteen years of my life, he never really paid for anything! He paid all the bills for a "short" while and then somehow we were about to lose everything we worked hard for. Thank God I am a strong woman because I was able to pull us out financially before the damage was too much to be repaired. Then I found he had another family on the side and that was where our funding was going. So my dear A.J. is history and on the emotional side, again, I am too strong to be upset over it. Instead of being a weeping willow, I went through another flowering period. His leaving was the best thing to happen to me! I am happy in my strongness,

I've gained a little more femininity and I am dating kinda sorta. Marlon is a great guy (and my boss) and as a friend he feeds my emotional side well. But I guess it is better to keep it on the professional level as he is my boss. When we are together its a few laughs and then its back to business. Its ok, I guess but I'm not wishing on stars to go further. There's other fish in the sea, I'm sure.

Sheppard is nice, but he's married! He makes me feel attractive, and feminine. He doesn't mind me being strong, intelligent or talented. The downside though; first and foremost, *he is married*, sometimes snorts coke, drinks all the time and is a die hard skirt chaser. Thousands of suspicions rise to the top every time I'm with him but I'm loving the attention regardless of his faults. And yesterday, I did run out of toilet paper, and I was so strapped for cash that I couldn't even pay for a 69 cent roll. But he must have sensed my distress when he dropped by as he gave me a twenty and came to my rescue! Does this mean I finally made it into the feminine ranks I so desperately want to join? Was it my womanly wiles or just being myself that caused this to happen? I don't know which it was and may never know; but I hope this continues because for once, I want to be a taker instead of a giver. I want to know what it is like to be pampered and shop for clothes I can't afford. I just want to be "kept" just like everybody else.

THE LADIES OF
APHRODITE'S COURT

Mrs. Rachens the principal of Crawley school introduced newly appointed teacher, Mr. Peter Sauls to his assistant, Ms. Eliza Jackson in the Learning Support class. These children were sixth, seventh and eighth graders who nobody was brave enough to teach except for their teacher, Mrs. Booker who was now seriously ill.

This group had gone through eleven subs in eleven days and were trying their best to build a reputation of being the baddest class in the school. So far, the little hellions were succeeding until now. Mr. Sauls was young, black and very friendly. Ms. Jackson on the other hand was very stern and can be really mean if she wanted to. She let it be known to him and the students that she could not be easily scared away and he told them the same thing despite his fear of the more tougher students. Right away they got them to do the assignments that the other subs were afraid to give them. It wasn't long that Sauls and Jackson were a great team and the children were back on track with their education. They became good friends and were never too far away from each other's side. Children and staffers alike were convinced that they had a thing going on. But it was not so as he was soon to be married and she was already married and ten years older than he. They respected each other as colleagues and as friends until one day a woman named Sasha seemed to appear out of thin air. She started bogarting Sauls and making Jackson feel as if she were invisible. Jackson even asked him if he were seeing Sasha but he said no.

But she continued to rule over him as if she were his girlfriend or wife. Jackson had the sneaking suspicion Sasha was trying to edge her out of Sauls's picture. After awhile Jackson grew tired of it and decided to hang around less with Sauls as he was totally under Sasha's spell. Jackson wasn't jealous of this but she didn't like being treated as if she were a fifth class citizen. Jackson wanted to teach Sasha a lesson but wasn't too sure as what to do. She knew every woman in the place was talking behind her back about her relationship with Sauls and just shrugged it off. Then again out of the blue a new person all of a sudden wanted to be Jackson's friend. Her name was Melinda and she was too friendly for Jackson's taste; she had never seen this Melinda before and here she was trying to be a friend. Jackson had a sneaky suspicion that this girl was spying on her and wanted to know if she was attached to Sauls in any way. And what better way to get information out of someone than the old "I come in peace ploy." Jackson was no fool and went along with the gag as she knew there were others around who were at the other end of this. And sure enough, Melinda revealed that she had a crush on Sauls. Jackson tired being the topic of the day and decided that she'd help Melinda get her feelings across to Sauls and, to get Sasha mad at someone else besides her. She knew it was a gamble to work along side an enemy, but figured she was smart enough to get out of the situation when the time came. She was clever and let her enemies believe she was stupid when in actuality it was they that came off stupid.

It wasn't long before her plan was put into action and Sauls seemed enamored by Melinda. He watched her every move and when his car broke down, he charmed his way into her life and carpooled with her everyday. This troubled Sasha greatly and she was quite jealous. This troubled Sasha so much that she had to confront Melinda. The shit had finally hit the fan, and while Melinda was in the the Discipline Room helping Paula and Sheela, she walked into a territory she knew nothing about and started a "cat fight" with Melinda. Sasha smugly said a frostily hello to the other ladies who of course didn't like her either. They barely mumbled a response and watched intently as Sasha went over to where Melinda was sitting.

She said, "So I hear you have some sort of problem with me. I came here to find out what it is and whether or not we can solve this." Melinda smirked, "Yes, I do have problem with you. First of all, you have no couth. Every time Mr. Sauls says anything to me, you have a conniption over him. It's a free country and until he tells me otherwise whether you and he are an item, then butt out." Sasha was shocked but cool. She replied, "Mr. Sauls and I are friends that's all and I don't fight over men anyway." "Could've fooled me Missy." said Melinda. With that, Sasha shook her head and walked away saying, "I'm too big of a person to come down to your petty level." As she walked away she heard the other ladies chiming in, "yeah she's big alright!" "Ooh! She's got a nerve to talk about petty!" "Who the fuck do she think she is?" "nobody to me evidently!" said Melinda. They all laughed at her remark and continued to gossip about Sasha.

As she left the room she bumped into Sauls who was rushing in to get a glimpse of Melinda before she left for the day. She took him by the arm and lead him away from his destination; as they walked down the corridor, she questioned him about what was going and he denied everything. "Naw baby, see I'm just being me. You know I like to talk to my lady friends; ain't nothing happening between me and anybody." Sasha wasn't convinced and for days after that, things grew tense and she had to know for sure whether it was true. She had already broken up Jackson's friendship with him and felt it was her crowning victory. She had alienated Jackson so well that she didn't even want to be seen with them. Sasha derived pleasure seeing Jackson standing alone on the busstop waiting for a bus in the hot sun instead of riding with them in Sauls's air conditioned car. She found it easy to make him laugh at Jackson even though he knew it was wrong to poke fun at the one person who helped him with his teaching career. But he couldn't figure out why Jackson took it so hard. They didn't mean any of the things they said or did. But Jackson didn't see it that way, she didn't like being the butt of every joke or having her life examined as if she were a science experiment. Melinda watched their cruelty and felt sorry for Jackson and offered her a lift home. Sauls questioned her about that and Melinda told him about himself and of how Sasha had come down on her sometime ago. Deep down he delighted in this sort of thing; he had all these women jumping through hoops and had no regard of who would get hurt.

One day, his car had to be put in the shop and Melinda came to his rescue since she found that they didn't live to far away from one another. So now the carpool consisted of Jackson, Sauls and her three children. Sasha was put out! Everyday at 2:45 she would ask Jackson whether or not Sauls was riding with Melinda or riding the bus with her. Jackson always told her she didn't know but of course she knew Sauls hated riding the bus and would choose a free ride anyday. Another rift developed between Melinda and Sasha and it soon escalated into a fist fight. After the fight, Melinda lost interest in Sauls as this was getting too deep for her and was getting tired of Sauls's God's gift to women attitude. After awhile she stopped hanging around everybody. Sauls and Sasha were an inseparable team again and continued to alienate Jackson further. Once they found out through "the Grapevine" that Jackson's marriage was on the rocks, they jeered her like little children that had nothing else better to do every time they saw her. Then Jackson became tired of their guff and she finally told them off. She told Sauls she regretted ever helping him with his career and that without her guidance and experience the students in the Learning Support class would've eaten him alive and as for Sasha, she said, "I have one word that describes you perfectly Sasha, "MOO". "Are you calling me a cow? How dare you!" Sasha screeched in disbelief. Jackson replied coolly, "If the hoof fits, wear it!" And with that she left them to contemplate her discussion. And sure enough, as time passed and Mrs. Booker returned to her position, he was given his own class and as Jackson predicted, he was devoured by the students. He put in a request to the principal for Jackson to be his assistant, but Mrs. Rachens was aware of what had happened and his attitude toward women, and so she sternly denied his request. Sasha got her just desserts too as her schedule was changed and the situation she had to handle was a rough one. She was constantly being threatened or dodging punches by the violent students in her charge. Sauls and Sasha's friendship also deteriorated because he realized that in losing Jackson as a friend and mentor he only gained a back biting complaining loud mouth who caused him alot of grief in the end. Meanwhile Jackson prospered despite now being divorced as she had a met a new male friend on the bus and soon was dating him. Life was good again and for the first time in her life Jackson was not the object of someone else's negative gossip and she was the victor in the Crawley school's stupid little soap opera.

It Should've Been Me

My best friend Leland is getting married. He is marrying Heather in 36 hours, 30 minutes and 27 seconds. So he threw a meet and greet party for all the participants and attendees. The eating, drinking, mingling and the forming of new friendships went on well after 1 a.m. and he invited me to stay over because the other guests were from out of town and he was too soused to drive. But he invited me without the consent of Heather, even though she didn't say anything about the situation, I could tell this was awkward. So here I am sleeping on an air mattress in their spare bedroom, harboring a secret love for him and wanting to share his bed.

As everyone settled in and all was still in the house, I lay awake on that air mattress listening to his snore. It was loud but somehow I felt comforted as I knew it was coming from him. When he is overly tired, his snore becomes rhythmic and cute as a baby's snore. Finally I let these sounds lull me to sleep and I dreamed she was not in this picture. I was awakened several minutes later as I felt as if were someone standing over me, I opened my eyes to see Leland. "What's the matter?" I asked and he said he missed me. I laughed and told him to go back to sleep; the only one he should be missing right now was Heather. Then I rolled over and bid him good night. But instead of leaving, he got onto the air mattress and straddled me. I said, "What the hell do you think you're doing? Get off of me!" He replied, "Nothing that you haven't been thinking about all these years I've known you; I want to give you what you want and what I've dreamed of too." Oh how I've longed to hear those words! But we chose years ago to remain friends after a disastrous attempt at having a romantic relationship and since then I kept my feelings hidden. I never realized that he felt the same way and now it was too late; he is marrying Heather in 36 hrs. "Regardless of how I feel about you Leland, I can't do this; we've made our choice and this is wrong." I said trying my best to pry him off of me. He replied, "Tonight, you sparkled as if I were seeing you for the first time and my heart beat only for you. Despite being pinned down by droll guests, I followed you with my eyes and when I couldn't see you, it troubled me. And the thought of you traveling alone on the subway hurt me and the thought of you sleeping over, excited me." I was moved by this but still the fact remained he was getting married to the woman sleeping in the next room. I really wanted him bad and that age old thrill of getting caught in the act intrigued me for a second; but my conscience just would not let me enjoy the moment.

He kissed me and I kept fighting and protesting; but he was persistent and touched that space only he knew about that drives to the point of no return. Despite my protests, my reserve waned and I soon gave in. It was bittersweet as he took me there . . . I wanted this so much for so long and the time was now. I couldn't hold back any longer and neither could he as our breathing took on that rhythmic beat as it matched our movements. I began to cry as my conscience screamed at me for allowing this to happen. He kissed my tears away and then I felt his tears as I returned each kiss as his conscience was screaming at him too. At the end, we lay together crying over the lost opportunities during our ten years friendship; lost opportunities because of our fear of the negative outcomes that sometimes happen when people fall in love. Then we saw the first breaks of sunlight creep through the window and we smiled. We kissed longingly as we knew this was our first and last time to be together and it was almost time for Heather to get up to begin her day. He grinded me sweetly as a memento of what was and went into the bathroom to clean himself up before returning to Heather.

I lay on that air mattress watching the sun come to its full bloom and listened to the morning birds sing songs that I never heard sound so bright and new. This spiritual moment was broken when I heard Heather's voice cooing to him and the bed squeaking frantically. I was jealous but I wondered, where did he get the stamina to do it again so soon after our encounter? Then I heard her say, "it's alright honey, we'll try again later." I smiled and gave myself a pat on the back. Afterwards I heard her footsteps nearing the back room, I pretended to be asleep as she poked her head in the room. She said, "wow, Dee is really zonked out! Good thing she did stay over, she was too tired to travel." Then she got herself together and went to work. I waited for an hour after she left before I prepared to shower; I was hoping to run into Leland and prayed she didn't have to return to the house for anything. He had the same idea and we showered together, sharing what little time we had left. It was noon when he drove me home and we departed from another; all through the day I walked in a dream as well as the next day and then came wedding day. I tried to be brave, but I couldn't as I cried uncontrollably making people believe I wept tears of joy and happiness for the couple; but in reality I cried because it should've been me.

CARTOON

Damn! I am commissioned to draw a cartoon for this syndicated news rag and I can't come up with a single storyboard. My cartoon is supposed to be everything that a tired mind enjoys after reading about all the sadness in the world. But no, my creativity is blocked! No pictures of smart ass rabbits being chased by a goofy wolf, nor do pictures of precocious Dennis the Menace types cross my mind. God, I am so stumped! Maybe if I watch a little TV for awhile an image will inspire me in some way.

Well, I watched the boob tube for an hour and by doing so I became more depressed as I realized just how lonely and boring my life is! There's no handsome man giving me flowers nor giving me a diamond just because, no good looking friends who like to frolic at the beach or sitting at the table playing a goofy game, laughing and having fun. God I wish life was like a TV commercial! Mr. Clean would be here everyday, cleaning my house and because he's been such a hunky piece of Americana for decades, I'd reward him with a change in his job description and allow him to become friendly with his female clients. Raid Roach spray would have a duo use, as it would be used for eliminating criminals too! Instead of mace or pepper spray to deter a foe, use Raid Roach & Criminal Deterrent to eliminate your attacker! Problem with that is, it would be too widely marketed and anyone could buy it, including criminals! And as for those food ads, I'll just eat a gallon of Breyers all natural Mint Chocolate Chip Ice Cream. Gee, if this were a commercial, life wouldn't get any better than this!

So, here I am at my computer; I just got through playing two games of Nanosaur, five games of Vegas poker and two games of

You Don't Know Jack; wow what a thrill fest but at least I was busy, but still no cartoon idea. I switch applications and open my AppleWorks Draw program and as I am staring at a blank page with my fingers drumming on the keys of my keyboard, something flashes in my mind. I see a face of someone, a face of someone I am sure I've never seen before and I am questioning myself of why I saw this vision of perfection. Is my subconscious mind trying to tell me something about this person who may have crossed my path somewhere and I had forgotten? Oh I don't know, but before I realized it, that face is now a graphic on my screen. His skin color is not the rosy pink color of Caucasionoid pigment, it's a light orangy/apricot color which looks like tanned or light complected Afro centric skin. Next thing I know, I completed his entire body frame and on my screen now is a very handsome studly male. **Woof!!!** I never knew I had the talent to draw the human form with such detail as silly animated caricatures are my thing and here and now this beautiful man sits before me on my computer screen.

I sat there for what seemed to be hours staring at him wondering what to do next. Then as I gazed into his deep brown eyes, he seemed to beg for me to name him; so I christened him Eriq-Michael D'lakenta. The graphic seem to brighten as if to let me know he was pleased with his name and I was pleased to have gained his approval. With all this joy going on, I was now deeply inspired to continue drawing. I drew scenes and backgrounds for Eriq-Michael so he could be more than just a picture on a screen. I gave him a beautifully furnished home with a garage; a hot, sporty car, parents, siblings and friends. I even drew scenes of places he likes to hang in and gave Eriq-Michael a life!

It was like playing with color forms as I cut and pasted and placed him in many of the scenarios I had created. But around midnight, I noticed my dear Eriq-Michael seemed sad; so I drew him a beautiful girlfriend but he didn't seem satisfied. So I drew him a dog and a cat to keep him company whenever friends and girlfriend wasn't around, still, he wasn't satisfied. I placed him in a job situation where he was the boss making big bucks, and still, he wasn't satisfied and no matter how many times I erased that maudlin look off his face, it mysteriously returned. I was truly amazed by this and pondered what was going on, then I was startled by my grandfather clock as it chimed at 3 a.m. I decided to shut down my IMAC and hit the hay. I heard the computer's engine whine as it shut down, but mere seconds later it restarted itself and opened the AppleWorks application to the last page of where I stopped in Eriq-Michael's life story. He stood there in a romantic garden scene I hadn't drawn and his gesture was one I hadn't mastered yet. My heart raced in fear while my mind rationalized that I overextended myself and that I'm dreaming or having some sort of fantasy and I'll wake up any moment and have a good laugh. Then I went to shut down my computer again but warm, firm human hands came through the screen and grabbed mine! I looked at the screen and Eriq-Michael's form was no longer a flat graphic. He was real! Then he pulled me into the computer screen. I screamed in terror as I was held fast by his hands as I floated past the computer monitor's circuitry and landed in the AppleWorks draw page with him. He let go as he said, "Welcome to my world." "What the hell is going on here? How did you do that? No. no . . . haha wrong question . . . **why** did you do that?" I yelled quite in a panic. He smiled sweetly, "the answer is a simple one; I'm lonely." I started laughing out loud, "What did you say? *You're* lonely? Oh come on Eriq-Michael! I created you and this world; I gave you everything your heart desired, how could you be lonely?" He looked down at his feet like a shy little boy and replied, "You aren't in this world and I'm in love with you." I was in shock! He saw the look on my face and explained further; "in your world time moves in minutes, here, time moves in the frames you create. In other words, many years have lapsed here and through them all I watched you and fell in love." This was something right out of the Twilight Zone! How am I to exist here if I am the creator of it and how do I get back to the real world? The look on my face was grim but it all changed when he said, "You can leave when you want to but, first test your feelings for me before you go." I searched those brown eyes and saw that he was indeed serious. I replied, "Okay, how do I do that? I know you are just a fantasy and this is just a dream." He said, "That's not what your heart says. Stay with me until your grandfather clock chimes 9 a.m., if I can't prove my love and you find you don't feel the same, you will be sent back. But if you do love me, I want you to stay forever and I promise, you'll never be alone again." I weighed my options very carefully, one hand, I'd be living happily in cartoon land with every wish coming true but on the other, I'd be in the real world depressed as all hell and wishing my life was as interesting as those people in a commercial again . I kept weighing those options and still I couldn't make up my mind . . . Then Eriq-Michael snapped me out of my funk by reminding me that the clock was ticking and we didn't have much time for more contemplation.So I took him up on his deal even though I still couldn't believe this whole thing was happening. The scenes changed every hour and each mood was romantic as he poured his heart out to me in every frame! I was showered with gifts of every kind, we danced, he serenaded me, we laughed and kissed in the rain and had impromptu picnics when his job schedule took too much of his free time.

I felt sooo free and I've never felt so alive! Time passed rapidly here as the frames continued on and here in Eriq-Michael's time, two years had passed. But back in the real world . . . the **REAL** world . . . . my grandfather clock just chimed 7 a.m. I hadn't realized how close to the deadline I was as I hadn't been paying attention even though my grandfather clock's chime is quite loud. Then at the 8 o'clock chime, Eriq-Michael was now middle aged and he asked me to marry him. Without thinking and in a heartbeat, I said yes.

Then at 8:30 a.m., something strange happened . . . . At our wedding, my father, who has been dead for fifteen years, was now in perfect health and strength to give me away and all my relatives and friends from the real world were sitting in the pews along with my new cartoon friends as if this was natural.

Afterwards at the dazzling ballroom where our reception was held, Eriq-Michael held me close as we danced and I couldn't tear myself away from him . . . I swear his magic was working overtime! Then at 8:45 a.m (grandfather clock time); we honeymooned in Hawaii.

My grandfather clock chimed 9 a.m. and then I couldn't hear it anymore. As a matter of fact as I looked up toward the opening I came through, there was nothing but blankness. I guess my heart had made up my mind for me even before my mouth could tell. Again, something strange happened, our middle agedness reversed and we were young twenty somethings again and we no longer moved in frames, but in sequential time like in the real world. However, despite all this bliss, Eriq-Michael failed to tell me that once I've decided to stay, that fantasy becomes reality and the cartoon bliss ceases to be.

So, we love, have disagreements, learn to deal with each other's quirks, endure stressful situations, juggle career with family, pay taxes and still be happy. It's reality alright, but I'm still free as I'm no longer alone and if even if this doesn't work out, I'll start cartooning again and see where it will take me.

CHAPTER 2

DARK TALES

GUILTY CONSCIENCE

I've always been a rogue male. I see something in a skirt that looks tantalizing, instantly she is mine. I woo with the strength of tornado, charm with the softness of a baby's blanket and I leave no stone unturned in my quest to get that to that prized booty.

Well, I tell you there was this one woman I met on the job, that caught my eye and she seemed to like me too. As time went along we grew close and during a free moment away from prying eyes in my office, we almost got it on. But what stopped us was her reluctance after I virtually forced myself upon her and she had slapped me. The next day, I apologized and asked that we remain friends. She walked away in a huff and after that she snubbed me daily. I wasn't sure whether she had told anyone about our little tete et tete in my office, but I did some locker room talk with a few of the fellas I had become pals with. I didn't think nothing of her feelings as I assumed the guys could keep it to themselves and the gossip would remain between just us fellas. Even though it seemed this was the case, however, I walked on eggshells for months as I feared someone with loose lips would sink my ship.

A year later, my female friend was promoted to manager and given an office. I was proud of her and offered words of congratulations but she just snubbed me more. Then one day, I was asked to get some office supplies out of a supply closet adjacent to her office. In that closet, I found it to be very roomy and it had windows that were a few feet below the ceiling. I was curious to find out what these windows looked out onto, so I stood on a small book case to reach them. They looked directly down into her office and as I watched her go about her business, I was totally intrigued by her again as her every movement just made me horny all over. And as the days went on, I began to find time to go to that isolated closet to get my daily fix of her. It got to the point where whenever she wore anything that showed her cleavage or wore a dress or skirt that showed how gorgeous her legs were, I'd be in that closet masturbating my brains out. Thank God that closet seemed sound proof because a couple times, I got quite noisy. This went on for some time and I no longer worried about the rumors I had started; nor had anyone else. I guess the thrill of the rumor had to die down sometime and I spent less and less time with the fellas and more and more time in that closet.

One day, her in box was so full, she couldn' t get rid of the paperwork fast enough. As soon as she got rid of a stack, a new stack arrived to take its place. Then I overheard her tell somebody she was staying late to work on those papers, and I decided to stay late too; thinking I could get a good rub on. Well, while I was in my hiding place, three guys came into her office to talk to her. They were the night janitors and they engaged her into a polite conversation while they went about their duties. Then I got a weird feeling something was up; her office was small and doesn't take three people to clean it. Although she was talking to them, she was very engrossed in her work and may not have noticed that they were circling her like a pack of hungry vultures. Suddenly one of them turned out the lights and locked the door, another grabbed her from behind and put a plastic bag over her head, while the third guy hit her. Despite the shades being drawn, it wasn't that dark in there as the windows still offered some late afternoon light and I could see their every movement as they prepared her for this heinous act. They knocked all her stuff off her desk, stripped her from the waist down and stretched her out on it, bounding her arms and legs in place with duct tape and with computer cables. When they finished setting up, they took the bag off her head and I could see that she was still unconscious while the guys just stood there gawking at the sight before them. Even though this scene bothered me, I was turned on as if I were watching a porno flick and gawked too. The first guy opened her blouse and took a pen knife to cut the bra and when those puppies spilled out I nearly gave myself away, fortunately, the men were too overjoyed by the sight to hear me. I watched as the first guy reveled in her breasts before dropping his pants. I was taken aback to see him apply a condom to himself and then work himself into her as his lips caressed every inch of her chest area. Oddly enough, I was envious and wanted to be in his place as minutes pass and he climaxed fast and rough. When he pulled out, he was dazed and muttered, "sweet". He took off the condom, wiped himself with a baby wipe and dressed. He said, "I'm going to the men's room to get rid of this. Duct tape her mouth before she comes to." By then I was about to cream myself, so I let it out and sprayed the wall. What a disgusting thing to do, I usually have tissues handy but this happened too quickly. After I calmed myself, I decided this was wrong; I wanted to get out there and find some help but then again, I was curious as to what the other guys would do.

The second guy, took some wipes and cleaned her. Then he licked her pubic area, tasting her and baby wipe juice. When it was wet to his liking, he too applied a condom then entered slow and rhythmically as if this was a scene from an orchestrated romance novel. I felt horny again as it was beautiful how he did it; but when it was time for him to come, he thrusted beastly and the romance was over. He came hard like he hadn't had none in a long while and I came to the sickening conclusion that I liked watching people do it. My manhood tingled but it wasn't ready yet; and by the time the third guy was up, it was jumping and ready for action. The third guy looked mentally slow and because he was huge, he broke three condoms before he got it on right! I thought I was well endowed, but this guy had a fucking trophy! Then she began to stir and when she opened her eyes she tried to scream but couldn't. Her eyes told it all and that look replayed in my mind as it reminded me of our little caper in my office. What I did was no different than this and suddenly my erection was gone as guilt took it away. Meanwhile, the third guy forced that humongous thing in like a square peg in a round hole. He banged til I could hear him slapping against her and she became so dazed, her eyes looked funny and her skin went pale as if all her blood was being drained away. When he climaxed, he roared like a fierce beast and withdrew harshly. I gasped in horror as upon his exit, blood spewed forth like a freshly dug well. When he saw this, he ran to the door to call the others, who were in the hallway taking a smoke. When they saw the blood on him and rushed back into the room to survey the scene, they hollered, "what the fuck did you do?" "why is she bleeding?" And he kept saying, "Stop yelling at me!! I didn't do anything you didn't do!!"

Despite the seriousness of this scene, I felt like I just watched The Three Stooges in a snuff film! But meanwhile my friend was suffering and here I was watching and doing nothing about it. Just when I got up enough nerve to get down and get help, I saw the first guy pull out a huge blade and shove it into her heart. I was in shock and felt sick but I dare not let myself be known now as I might be next. I continued to watch as they tried to make the scene look like a break in; making sure there wouldn't be any evidence that could link them to this. As they left, I could tell they felt confident they left no evidence; but then again, they weren't aware of me.

I stayed in that closet for an hour after the killers were gone; I wanted to make sure I could make a clean getaway so I could call the police. But as I sat in that closet of semen stains and office supplies, I felt fear. Not of the guy with the blade nor his brothers, but fear of being accused. If anyone found out about what I was doing in this closet day after day, my secret would be found out and I would be labeled a pervert and a coward for life. I contemplated leaving the scene, but evidence of my being there was all over that closet. I weighed the pros and cons of it all, my mind said to clean the wall and pretend nothing happened. But my heart said, cleaning the closet can't clean my conscience of witnessing a murder and not doing anything about it. So I listened to my heart and soon my mind concurred with its reasoning; so I found some cleaning stuff in the closet, cleaned the areas I soiled and left to go to my office to call 911.

The cops arrived, I told them everything except about my voyeuristic escapades but that didn't dissuade their forensics department from running tests on every inch of that closet. There was a spot I missed and of course their stupid tests proved I did more than just retrieve office supplies. Not only did I help in apprehending my friend's murderers, I helped myself right into jail sentences for stalking, sexual harassment, vandalism, indecent exposure, invasion of privacy and was fired for misconduct on the job. Despite all of this, there is a bright side; I came to grips with the fact that it was my own loose lips and nobody else's that sank my ship and caused the death of my friend. I've heard, the truth will set you free and because it has, my conscience is clear now.

BEVERLEIGH'S OBSESSION

Miriam and Everrett Dansfield were having marital problems because after fifteen years of wedded bliss, infidelity had entered their relationship and threatened to end their once secure bond. Everrett had secretly rekindled his affections for Beverleigh Stewart, who he had once dated in college. They were reintroduced at the Jefferson Middle School where Miriam and Everrett are instructors. Beverleigh was assigned there as a reading resource teacher and hadn't wasted any time making her presence known to Everrett.

Miriam had a deep suspicion that something was going on, but she had no real proof. One day, her curiosity got the best of her and she asked him if there was someone else in his life; he reacted by smacking her. She didn't expect to be knocked on her ass, but it was enough proof to quell her suspicions. After that incident, they separated and Everrett secretly moved in with Beverleigh. But he did not inform Miriam of his new residence and at this point, Miriam was too angry to care.

Despite shacking up with Beverleigh, Everrett was unhappy; she did anything and everything a man could ever want in his wildest dreams, but where was the tenderness? He missed those quiet evenings in the summer, when he and Miriam would sit on the rooftop of their home, cuddling and sipping iced tea on a blanket beneath starry sky. And so, after a couple of months with Beverleigh, he decided to go back to his wife to salvage what was left of their marriage. Beverleigh was not pleased about this and vowed to get him back one way or another. Beverleigh was so angry the day Everrett left, that she virtually destroyed her apartment. "Not again! That bitch always seems to get him away from me!! How could he want that dried up old thing! She can't do the things I do; oh noo, she would be too repulsed, if she had to do the things I do to satisfy you." She paced for hours muttering to herself as she recalled their college days and how easy it was to catch Everrett's eye. But what she didn't know then was that he wasn't as naive as she had perceived. She remembered how smitten he was and he did anything for her as long as the sex was great and hot. Then out of nowhere, came Miriam. She was quiet, bookish and shy; the all American girl, next door type. A true pure Polly and Beverleigh hated her guts. All the guys flocked to her and it was Beverleigh's opinion that Miriam was too plain to be receiving such attention. Rumor had it that she was a virgin, and it was open season, as the men on campus were on the hunt and Everrett was no exception. She remembered over hearing a conversation between Everrett and his pal, Derrick about a bet to see who'd be the first to go all the way with Miriam. It was the old wham bam, thank you mam, but despite never getting to do anything sexual with Miriam, Everrett fell in love with her anyway. He hadn't expected this and it complicated his relationship with Beverleigh. She also remembered when she gave a pool party at her parent's condo. She invited Everrett and mostly all his male friends to the party; it was going well until he walked in with Miriam on his arm. Beverleigh tried everything in her power to gain his attention. She tried to be civil but couldn't hold her tongue or temper back much longer and asked to see him in the kitchen. As they passed a buffet table full of exotic foods, he asked "Who are you trying to impress this time?" She screeched, "Why is she here?!" He smirked at her agitation, "Why? Are you jealous?" "You son of a bitch! How dare you dump me for that fluff!" He laughed, "Why do you care? You've slept with every man here! It was fun in the beginning, but I need a little more than having my dick sucked. She's one hell of a lady and has class and dignity, all you have is a great body and some good moves in bed. Frankly my darling, that's not enough to keep nor satisfy me." He winked at her and walked out of the kitchen to rejoin Miriam. After a few minutes of crying and sulking, she went out to the pool. Every time she swam close to the couple, she made sure to make them uncomfortable. When she saw Everrett leave to go to the bathroom, she saw a chance to get even with Miriam while she was unattended. Beverleigh said sweetly as she got out of the pool, "Hi, having a good time?" Miriam felt uneasy; she was not aware

Beverleigh and Everrett were a couple, but had a gut feeling that Beverleigh was up to no good. So she made an excuse to go inside and as she took a few steps, Beverleigh shoved Miriam into the pool and dove in too trying to keep Miriam down, but Miriam was stronger than she thought and broke free from her grasp and surfaced. By then all the guests's attention was to the pool as Beverleigh pretended to help Miriam. Soon Everrett caught sight of Miriam sputtering and coughing, he ran to her side to help along with the other guests. Beverleigh said feigning concern, "She tripped and I thought she hit her head." Everrett wasn't fooled and Miriam knew her enemy. Beverleigh seethed with anger as her plan failed to get results and he called her that night threatening her to stay away from Miriam. That was the ultimate humiliation as she never forgot his harsh words.

To this day, she was still seething, plotting to find a way to get him back into her life. But the more she thought about it, the angrier she became and angrier still, because there weren't any more things for her to throw. Her apartment was in shambles, she started to cry and decided to clean up the mess she made, "I'll get my way someday Everrett Ross Dansfield and you will love me, you can bet on it!"

May 14, 1992

As they drove to work, Everrett hadn't spoken a word to Miriam as he thought over the events that had taken place yesterday afternoon with Beverleigh. She came into his science lab with a big grin on her face with her body swaying to catch his attention but he wasn't impressed. It had been three weeks since their affair ended and she still was trying to change his mind. She went to hug him, but he pushed her away and told her that their affair was over. He remembered how hurt and angry she was and could still feel the heat from her body as her blood boiled as she seethed with rage. She cursed and spat at him, but the words that stung him most were about Miriam. "She doesn't appreciate you the way I do! She only wants you for a trophy; for fifteen years she's been fronting, pretending to love you . . . why are you still with that bitch?" He looked her straight in the eye, "Because she's everything you are not." She slapped him as hard as she could, "I swear Everrett, you'll pay for this!!! Nobody dumps me and gets away with it!" He said sarcastically, "where have I heard that one before?" She stormed out, slamming the door behind her. The sound echoed in his mind as he drove and wondered how much of her threats were true.

As their car turned into the school's parking lot, Miriam was tempted to ask him what was going on, but she feared it would cause another rift between them so she said nothing and gave him a goodbye kiss before getting out of the car. She hated whenever he got into one of his moods, she always felt so left out of his life. Maybe he was having second thoughts about their marriage; she hoped not as she wasn't so sure she would be able to handle the loneliness after he was gone. During the time of their separation, she was angry but deeply depressed and every time Everrett brought up the topic of divorce, her heart felt as if it would break into a million pieces. Then she dismissed that thought, "I'm getting paranoid in my old age." and decided that he might not have slept well the night before.

Miriam's morning was a disaster as her first and second period classes, were very disruptive. By her lunch time, she had a tension headache the size of Texas and fished into her purse to find Motrin tablets. After popping some, she closed her door, turned the lights off and returned to her desk to put her head down to rest. She set her watch's alarm to go off in forty-five minutes for the fourth period session. As the Motrins took effect, she slept so soundly that she did not hear Everrett come in to leave a surprise on her desk.

Forty-five minutes passed quickly and she awoke as the fourth period bell and her watch's alarm sounded in unison, and to her surprise, she found a dozen of mixed colored roses in a pretty crystal vase sitting on a corner of her desk. The card read:

> Dearest Miriam:
> I apologize for my behavior of this a.m. I would like to make it up to you, so how's about a romantic dinner on the river's finest dining ship, The Spirit Of Philadelphia tonight? My treat of course, what do you say love? Buzz my lab if you forgive me and if your answer is yes.
>
> Love—Everrett—

She smiled as she walked over to the wall phone to ring his lab. There was a loud buzz and then his deep baritone voice answered; "Science lab, Mr. Dansfield speaking." She cooed into the receiver, "Hi love, my answer is yes to both questions!" He replied, "Great! We'll discuss the details later. Love ya." "I love you too!" She hung up the phone and thought, "he does love me! And to think I worried myself for nothing!" The rest of Miriam's day was just as crappy, but it didn't get her down because she had a hot date with her husband. "There will be no papers to mark tonight!"

While Everrett was on his way out of the building, he passed Beverleigh in the hall. He read her thoughts, "it's not over yet." He interjected a thought of his own hoping she'd pick up on it. "It's over bitch; don't try any tricks or else." As he walked into the warm afternoon sunshine, he channeled all his thoughts on his plans for the evening. Even though he wanted his plans to be just right, they took a detour and never made it to The Spirit Of Philadelphia.

In the weeks that followed, the Dansfields acted as if they were newlyweds. They were a happy couple once more and had high hopes to remain so for many years to come. Beverleigh had other ideas though, her hate for Miriam grew intense as well as her yearning for Everrett. She wanted him so bad that she could almost taste him; then a devious plan formed in her mind to get him back; Everrett Ross Dansfield was going to love her one way or another.

Monday, June 1, 1992

As Everrett was enroute to his lab on the third floor, he had to pee really bad. It was lucky for him that the lab was equipped with a small bathroom tucked in a corner of the back of the room. He ran into the lab, slamming the door so hard that the glass cracked. His only goal for the moment was to get into that bathroom asap! There were only two men's rooms in the place and neither located anywhere near his lab. "Thank God for the science lab and its many conveniences!" he said while rushing into the mid-sized bathroom. The bathroom was bathed in semi-darkness as light was offered from a tiny window and if he had left the door open, light from the lab itself would have revealed Beverleigh's hiding place. He unzipped his fly, whipped out his penis and whizzed like no one on Earth ever has; Beverleigh hid in the shadows waiting for her chance to make her move as she watched his silhouetted movements. When the time had come, she eased behind him carefully and stood by the door, making sure it was locked. Suddenly, he gave a loud sigh of relief indicating that he was done; zipped his pants then leaned over the sink to wash his hands.

When he turned to leave, he came face to face with her. Before he could move or utter a sound, she gave him the most passionate, French kiss she could give and for reasons he couldn't explain, he did not resist. He was lost to her whims and hadn't realized she had pinned him to the wall and had pulled his pants and underwear down to his ankles. She knelt before him, he felt the warmth of her mouth gently surround his penis. He gave in to all the sensations and soon ejaculated. She spat into the toilet and said, "can she make you feel the way I do Everrett? This may repulse Miss Priss, but you love it and can't get enough . . ." She kissed his neck and cooed into his ear softly, "admit it Ev, you want me and you want me bad!" He said nothing as he stared past her trying to control his urges. He thought, "Oh God, How could I have let this happen!?!" Finally he pushed her away, got dressed and he said quite gruffly, "Enough is enough! Get away from me before I break your fucking neck! It's over; nothing's going to change my mind." "Yeah right, like you didn't enjoy my little surprise just now. What is it about her, that keeps you bound? It can't be her pussy, cause you came just like a man who hasn't had none in a very long time! How long has it been since you and Prissy got it on? A week, a month, a year?" She giggled like his sex life was a big joke. He heard enough and backhanded her across the face releasing some of the swelling anger he felt in his soul. "Shut up you crazy bitch! Leave my lab, or I'm going to kick your fucking ass!" She scoffed, "Is that the tone of voice that slays Prissy? Well, you don't scare me baby." She tried to kiss him but this time he lost control and choked her. "Fuck you bitch! If you ever come near me again, I'll kill you with my bare hands!" He threw her on the floor and stormed out. As she lay on the floor trying to catch her breath, she rubbed her neck, that'll be the day, and we'll see who kills who!"

That night, he was so filled with guilt that he went to bed early. As his head throbbed and would not let him rest, he popped four Valium hoping for some comfort. Miriam joined him but saw that he was irritated, so instead of prying, she decided to question him in the morning. The next day, Everrett felt like warmed over death as that woman really had him riled, and he hadn't a clue as to how to rid himself of her. It was true, he was addicted to her sexual prowess, but that was all. Miriam gave him everything; love, companionship and great sex. Unfortunately, it became routine but his love for Miriam was strong and he prayed for a miracle to get Beverleigh out of his life. This troubled him so much that he worked half of the day and left the car in the lot for Miriam. He left a message along with the car keys in her mailbox in the main office and trusted public transit to get him home. It was a long exhausting trip but he didn't care, as long as he was a great distance away from Beverleigh, he felt safe. But before heading for home, he hit every bar within a ten block radius, and by the time he reached the last bar enroute to home, he was totally smashed. After his second drink there, the bartender refused to give him more and just by luck, a neighbor saw him and coaxed him into going home and made sure Everrett drank enough coffee to sober up some. Everrett was sick as a dog but he didn't have any regrets about what he had done this day.

When Miriam arrived home, she found him lying in a pool of his vomit on the livingroom floor. She put her things away and looked at him with disgust; then went into the kitchen to retrieve cleaners, and a bucket of water. She returned to the livingroom armed with all these things and poured some of the water on him. He awoke out of his drunken stupor long enough for her to help him into the bathroom. She stripped him of his messy clothing, bathed him and put him to bed then prepared to take on the foul task.

As she cleaned the offensive mess, she did not know what to think about this new development; never in the fifteen years of their marriage had she seen him so drunk. Tomorrow, when he was feeling better, she planned to interrogate him and get to the bottom of this and she said out loud, "What brought this on?"

Morning came and they couldn't face each other; he was still feeling a little rocky and she was just mad. As they sipped their coffee at the kitchen table, the air in the room was so thick that you could cut it with a knife. Finally, Miriam spoke first despite the rising anger she felt. "What happened to you yesterday? Who or what, is making your life so damned miserable that you had to get drunk? The last time we had a problem, I didn't want to know her name, but today is a different story. I demand that you tell me who she is Rett!! I want whoever this bitch is, to leave us alone; no more lies because I can't continue to live like this!" He knew he was in hot water now, she called him Rett. God how he despised that nickname and the only time she called him that was when she was mad. His head raced wildly with pain, he cradled his head in his hands, sobbing, "I'm so sorry Miriam! I just didn't know what to do . . . it's like she's got a spell over me." Her anger made him feel uneasy, as he wasn't really sure of what she was capable of doing. He swallowed hard, "It's . . . it's Beverleigh Stewart." She looked as if she was about to explode. "Oh my God Rett, how could you do this to me? All these years, I thought you loved me . . . Why her?!" She was hysterical, he went to comfort her, but she pulled away. "Don't touch me! If she's that damned important to you, then, you can have her! I'll even grant you that divorce!" "No Miriam! I don't want a divorce, I want you! She means nothing to me, I swear!" He began to sob as he pleaded for forgiveness, she saw in his eyes that he was truly ashamed of his actions. She recalled how Beverleigh mistreated her in college and of how she had to bare the humiliation of being a professional colleague to her worst enemy. All these memories, thoughts, and emotions had come to a boiling point; she had nothing else to say to Everrett as he sat there, wallowing in self pity. She left the kitchen to take a shower and to get dressed. Before he could utter a word, she was out of the door and starting the car. The squeal of the tires awoke many of their neighbors and disturbed the birds in the trees as she sped down the road. Although her feelings were hurt, her anger was stronger and wasn't sure what she was going to do or say to Beverleigh, but she was certain it wasn't going to be pleasant.

At the school, she spied Beverleigh; Miriam barely stopped the car before getting out of it and ran inside the building to catch up with her. When she did, she tried to be calm so her anger wasn't so noticeable. But Beverleigh could see in Miriam's eyes that some thing was up. Miriam walked with her into an empty teacher's lounge and pretended to go in there to get a cup of coffee. To satisfy her curiosity, Beverleigh said, "So Miriam, what's up? What's on your mind?" Before she could speak, Miriam decked her with a strong right cross to the jaw, knocking her on the floor. Then she grabbed her by the collar and threatened her. "Stay away from Everrett bitch, or next time I won't be so fucking gentle!!" Beverleigh yelled back from the floor, "watch yourself Miss Prissy! You obviously don't know who you're fucking with!" Miriam smirked, "evidently, neither do you." She left the building with no notion to return to work that day. As she headed for home, she called Everrett from their cellular car phone and told him to stay put; they both were taking the day off so that they can put their marriage back on track again as this was war and she was determined to be victorious.

June 26th, 1992

The Last of School For Staff

Everyone was in a hurry to clean up their rooms and pack up supplies for September. The sooner they finish their tasks, the sooner they could start their vacations. The Dansfields were no exception; Everrett was busy putting away all his lab equipment as Miriam finished her room, but she still had a few papers to run off for the fall session. Miriam went to the copy room down the hall from her room but found it locked; so she decided to use the one on the fourth floor instead. After prepping the ditto machine for operation; she fished into her purse for her mini cassette player as listening to her music calmed her as this room always gave her the creeps. It was a quiet place, but it was too secluded from the other classrooms. It was dangerous to be alone at that end of the corridor because it always seemed dark and creepy and there were too many ways for someone with harmful intentions to gain access to the building. Miriam was aware of this but felt safe as long as she knew that there was other people on this floor beside her.

As the ditto machine made quick work out of the paper she fed into the paper tray, she changed the ditto master and filled the feeder tray again as she sang along with the tune that was playing on her cassette player. She was in a good mood; she and Everrett were to spend their entire summer vacation in the Poconos and she could hardly wait. Everything was already packed and loaded in the trunk of their car so there'd be no delay hitting the trail to the Poconos to have the time of their lives.

As she attended to the ditto machine, she could barely hear it clanking over the loudness of her cassette player nor did she hear the foot steps of another person. But what caught her attention was the sweet floral scent that now filled the room. Miriam's back was turned to that person and she shouted over her shoulders, "I'll be out of your way in a few seconds." While she was busy, the other person walked over to the tall lockers and took out a small axe, she crept back a little and when it was at the right angle and space to swing it, she brought down its sharpest edge down on Miriam's head. She felt searing pain as it shocked her system and dropped to the floor like a stone. The blow did not kill her but her body twitched and writhed on the floor as bone shattered and nerves were severed. Her headphones fell off her ears when she was struck and now she could hear her attacker's cruel laughter and the sound of the ditto machine clanking on. Her attacker rolled her over on her back so Miriam could see who did this to her. Everything was a blur and she could not see her attacker clearly as her eyes would not focus and as streams of blood poured into them, she wanted to scream for help but found that she was unable to; all she could utter was a silent, "God help me!"

Finally her attacker spoke, "Before I finish you off, I want you to know I've waited a long time for this. You thought you had the upper hand when you beat me up; but I'm keeping my promise to kill you!" Miriam's expression told of the fear that she could not voice as her attacker brought the axe down on her face. Blood splattered everywhere as her attacker continued to hack away at her face with the axe. She was not through with her yet as she admired the rings Miriam wore and decided that she should have them as the diamonds tempted her to take them. She tried to pry them off but the fingers were too swollen, so she pushed them as close to the knuckle as far as they could go and severed the fingers with the axe and threw the dismembered digits into the trash. She looked down at what was left of Miriam, "someone bashed your face in. Tsk, tsk, tsk." Then she kicked the bloody mass that was Miriam in the ribs and left with her stolen loot.

Everett finally put all the equipment away and locked his room; he went looking for Miriam as he hadn't seen nor heard from her in two hours. He went to the classrooms of her friends, but they had already left. He checked her classroom and found her belongings still hanging in the closet; he looked out the window into the parking lot and saw their car was still there. Then he remembered that she had told him earlier about running off papers. He ran up the stairs very eager to see his wife and midway into the empty hall, the sound of the ditto machine's gears grinding echoed off the walls. But he couldn't understand why that machine was making such a weird noise and this sound helped hasten his quest. When he reached it, he was immediately repulsed by the bloody display; he let out a loud wail and felt his lunch rise in his throat. He found the trash can and was sickened further by the sight lying in it. He couldn't hold back any longer; he felt as if he were throwing up his heart as well as his lunch. A deep dark sorrow quickly filled his once happy soul; he wanted to cradle her in his arms but the sight of the bloody mass that once was his beloved wife repulsed him too much to do so and ran out of the room to find help. He ran down four flights of stairs and into the main office on the first floor where the secretary and a few staffers were chatting. "Kristen! Call the police! Miriam's been attacked in the fourth floor copy room! Hurry!!" The secretary made the call as some of the staffers comforted him and others went to see the murder scene as Beverleigh quickly scooted by while everyone was distracted. She drove away and laughed out loud to herself as she felt confident she had committed the perfect crime, and was getting away clean.

Later that evening he called Beverleigh for consolation; she acted concerned but deep in her heart she laughed. Everett offered to her the keys to the cabin in the Poconos but she wouldn't take his offer unless he'd come too. He declined but insisted that she go and after finishing his conversation, he went into his study and pulled out of his desk drawer, a bottle of Jack Daniels he had been hiding from Miriam. (He had tendency to abuse alcohol and that worried

Miriam greatly; but she respected his privacy and never inspected his desk.) After swilling down half of the bottle's contents, he fell asleep, dreaming he was making love to her by the lake and smiled in his sleep as he could almost feel all the sensations their lovemaking would have brought. But suddenly, his dream faded away into the vision of the bloody mass that was the body of his wife. He awoke with a start, "MIRIAM!!!"

JANUARY 1, 1993

Beverleigh made herself available to Everrett as he had become such an emotional cripple and depended on her heavily. She didn't mind as she was delighted to share every moment with him and figured that sooner or later, he was going to ask her to marry him. She reveled in the fact that there was nothing to interfere with her marital plans and when she was alone at her home, she would sit at her bedside vanity and put on Miriam's rings. She imagined receiving the friendship ring on a Valentine's Day when they were still in college; the engagement ring sometime after their graduation and the wedding ring received at their very special Christmas Day wedding. Such perfect dreams and all she had to do now was to make them a reality.

APRIL 15, 1993

After attending an art exhibit at the Philadelphia Art Museum, Everrett took her on a romantic stroll around the surrounding area and led her into a large gazebo overlooking the Schuylkyll River. When they were finally alone in the gazebo, he got on his knees to propose and she shed tears of joy as she had waited for so long for this moment. Meanwhile as the couple embraced, the sun which had shined so brightly, was soon covered by dark foreboding storm clouds, which rolled in so fast that it seemed unnatural. But the couple was so engrossed by their romantic moment that they didn't care to pay the outside activity any mind. As they embraced, Beverleigh thought to herself, "Miriam must be turning over in her grave over this!"

MIRIAM'S RETURN

Hello my name is Celeste Holman and I'm a private detective. Yes, that's right, a female private detective; most people can't deal with that but on the whole, I really do a great deal of business. Believe me if you will, that I've had my share of the usual cheating spouses, alimony dodger cases as well as medical injury fraud and low brow corporate espionage. But nothing can compare with the strange case I am about to embark on; it's a year old murder case that hasn't been solved nor will it ever because everything was done so clean the police wrapped it up tighter than a drum; until now. This is my tale that I felt needed to be recorded if anything should happen to me while undercover so to speak. So here goes.

Yesterday, a woman bearing a striking resemblance to me came to my office and told me she was my sister. Of course I didn't believe her because my parents raised only two of us, myself and my brother Nathaniel, and as far as I know, there are no "on the side siblings" outside of my parent's very loving relationship. However, Mrs. Miriam Taylor-Dansfield provided old birth and adoption records that showed that we were infants when were adopted by different families. She was two and I was a mere three months when our parents were killed in a car accident. Our birth parents each were only children and had no other known living relatives that could take care of us; and so, we became wards of the state. This was very intriguing and I was glad to know that I had gained a sister; but what amazed me was the tale that she had spun afterwards which was the true reason for the visit. She said, she was dead. I nearly burst out laughing until she began to levitate just to prove her point; and just for a little more proof, she told me to look in the mirror behind me, all I could see was my own reflection! I thought it all to be a good magician's trick until she vanished before my eyes and after that I was convinced.

She gave me the details of what led up to her grisly murder and the name of her murderer was Beverleigh Stewart. She wanted me to help her seek revenge for this woman's misdeeds. A chill ran up and down my spine as I thought this was all so creepy; but as we talked, I felt a sisterly bond grow between us. I now felt bound to do this and so it was soon agreed; Miriam Dansfield was to rise from the grave in more ways than one.

JUNE 26, 1993

The Anniversary of Miriam's Death

It has been a year since that terrible day Everrett found his wife dead. He constantly wondered why he stayed on at Jefferson after such an ordeal, but he had no answer to his wonderment. He wished he had the answers to a lot of things but the questions after awhile just mounted and caused him to be more depressed as if her death occurred daily. And as the Dansfields packed for their vacation, a knock came at their door; Everrett opened it and was almost floored by the visitor's appearance. Puzzled by his reaction she said, "Are you alright sir?" "It's just you look like somebody I knew . . ." They smiled warmly and she said, "I've been told, everybody has a twin out there somewhere. Hi, I'm Celeste Holman and I just moved in next door and I was wondering if I could use your phone. The telephone company was supposed to have been here hours ago but they left me hanging." They shook hands, "Sure, come in. I'm Everrett Dansfield and welcome to the neighborhood." He escorted her to the telephone and made her comfortable in their home. Just then Beverleigh came downstairs, "who was at the door?" When she saw the woman, she almost fainted as Everrett introduced her to Miriam's double. "Beverleigh, this Celeste Holman, our new next door neighbor, and Celeste, this is my wife, Beverleigh." The women exchanged greetings but Beverleigh couldn't get over the remarkable resemblance Celeste had to Miriam, but Celeste was younger and had more appeal. After Celeste finished her call, Everrett escorted her out and watched as she went into her home. Beverleigh noticed him gawking, "Earth to Everrett! Everrett! This is your wife speaking, snap out of it!" He replied, "She looks just like Miriam . . ." "But she's not; so hurry up and finish packing so we can get going." She uttered while trying not to be upset over this new development.

Hours later, Celeste watched from her second floor window as the Dansfields drove down the road to their vacation spot. Then she closed her eyes and thought of Miriam. "Okay sis, nobody's here but me and you. What's next?" Miriam appeared, "excellent Celeste. You shook 'em up pretty good." "Especially the wife." said Celeste. Miriam laughed heartily, "She should be shaking, after all, I've come back to life!!"

SEPTEMBER 1993

The school year had begun and a new crop of faculty and students were to be bustling through the halls of Jefferson Middle School. The first day was for staff development and as an introduction ritual for the new members. To Everrett's joy and Beverleigh's dismay, they discovered that their new neighbor, Celeste Holman was to be Everrett's lab assistant. As Celeste chattered away at how great it was going to be working with them, Everrett was thrilled and Beverleigh wanted to kill her.

DECEMBER 1993

The Staff Christmas Party

At the staff party on the Spirit Of Philadelphia, everyone dressed in their holiday best and many were shocked to see each other looking so elegant. When Celeste took off her coat to reveal a very slinky, short black dress with a matching black choker, Everrett was mesmerized most of all as he was used to seeing her in tight jeans and big shirt covered by a lab coat. Her hairstyle and makeup added to her glamorous look and every male staffer flocked to her as she entered their section of the boat. They led her to a table and each man made sure they were sitting next to her in some way. All the women were jealous, especially Beverleigh. Celeste noticed all the dirty stares she received and decided she wanted to dance. She purposely chose Everrett, hoping this would give the other women a chance to mingle with the men. The music was uptempoed and Everrett danced like he was a pro. Beverleigh was shocked as she didn't know he could as he never took her dancing nor had he ever danced with her at home. The music changed to a slow romantic song, Celeste wanted to leave the dance floor; but he took her by the hand and drew her in close. He gazed into her eyes, transfixing her into his charms as he slowly brushed himself against her. She closed her eyes and gave in to the mood; but it all came to an abrupt halt as Beverleigh snatched him away. As to not make a scene, Celeste calmly walked to the Ladies' Room to cool down from his spell. As she looked in the mirror, Miriam appeared, "Good going Sis! Ol' Bev's madder than a teased pit bull!" "I can't do this; Everrett's falling in love with me and I'm afraid I'm falling for him too. This isn't an act anymore." "So? What's the problem? This helps to make it more convincing! Don't worry, whatever happens, I'll be there to share it all with you." "What do you mean?" "You'll see, when the time comes." She cut her transmission short as some women walked into the ladies room. Celeste returned to her colleagues and noticed Beverleigh was guarding Everrett like he was a piece of gold. But despite this, Everrett couldn't stop looking at Celeste, proving that the seduction was in full effect.

JANUARY 2, 1994

Celeste had a headache as the students worked her nerves. As she was on her way to the teacher's lounge, Beverleigh grabbed her. "Hey! What's wrong with you?" "Don't play dumb bitch! I saw what you did to my Everrett at the Christmas party! If I ever catch you near him again, I'll kill you!" Beverleigh walked away leaving Celeste hoping she would have the courage to carry on with her mission. But she put her fears and doubts away as she knew the plan was working and time to really stick it to Beverleigh and to bring her to justice.

Several weeks after Beverleigh's confrontation, Celeste played it cool around Everrett. But he couldn't take it anymore and during one of those brief moments they were alone in the lab, he took her in his arms and kissed her. She resisted at first and then told him, "not here Everrett, your wife will kill me if she knew how I felt about you." "Is that why you been avoiding me?" he asked. "Yes. Ever since the Christmas party, you've been on my mind, but I don't want to interfere with your marriage." "Don't worry, I'll find a way that we can be together." "I'm sure you will Everrett; but in the meantime, I've got experiments to set up." He watched her go about her work and his eyes fixed on her ass; "It's so uncanny how much she looks like Miriam; but Miriam's ass never looked like that!"

MARCH 21st, 1994

Beverleigh had the flu and was confined to bed rest for a week or more, giving Everrett and Celeste time to be together. During their lunch break, he locked the lab's door and led her into it's bathroom; as they kissed, Miriam's spirit possessed Celeste. As they continued, Everrett called out Miriam's name as they were climaxing and she delighted feeling him again.

After work, Everrett hummed as he drove home and was puzzled of what made their rendezvous in the bathroom so intense. Even though Beverleigh had all moves and techniques, Miriam was the one who really knocked his socks off and now here was Celeste with the same moves rocking his world and drawing him in deeper.

At home, he hadn't gotten in the house fully before he heard his wife's rasping voice. "Why are you so late? You stop off to see Celeste?" "No dear, I didn't stop off to do anything. An accident blocked the road and traffic was backed up for miles on the express way. Are you satisfied?" She didn't answer and he assumed she was going back to sleep. After hanging up his coat, he went into the kitchen to fix something to eat; he made soup and sandwiches and took a tray upstairs. He placed the tray upon the nightstand on her side of the bed, "are you feeling any better?" She snapped, "what the Hell do you think Dr. Kildare? What did you make for dinner?" He handed her meal to her, "I hope its to your liking." She tasted the soup and took a bite of the sandwich. "Its fine, get out of here so I can rest." "As you wish dear" as he closed the door behind him he replied, "bitch."

Moments later, Beverleigh heard their car door slam, she wearily went to the window and saw Everrett pull off with Celeste. As her anger grew fierce, her blood boiled, and she threw the tray of food at the window. She screeched, "No! I will not lose Everrett to some carbon copy of Miss Priss!" Suddenly her body was racked by a few hard coughs that took her strength. She crumpled upon the bed muttering between heaves, "she's dead meat, you just wait . . ."

Miriam was in her glory as she experienced his lovemaking, but felt selfish to keep doing this to Celeste but the feeling of being alive was too addictive to shake. She screamed in ecstasy as she could feel him explode within her sister's body and relished the delight as she heard him call out her name as he fed her his passion. He still loved her and that was the icing on the cake, but despite the successfulness of their plan and the happiness Miriam felt, Celeste regretted falling in love with Everrett. After all, she was a private detective on a case and falling in love was not part of the job description. She used that as an excuse while trying to maintain her objective as she grew weary of the possessions. However, Miriam was aware of her sister's thoughts and decided to possess her for as long as it took to make Beverleigh confess. But it was going to take time as she knew Beverleigh liked to perfect her plans before putting her murderous schemes in effect.

MARCH 30th, 1994

Beverleigh spent the day visiting her parents and when she got back, she found him gone. Although the hour was late, she looked out her window and noticed Celeste's car was gone from it's garage. Seconds later she heard Everrett's car pulling up and a few minutes afterwards she heard Celeste's piece of junk pull in. When Everrett entered the house, instead of throwing a tantrum, she kissed him passionately. This took him by surprise and he countered with the same passion as it was given. He lifted her into his arms and carried her up to their bedroom. But Beverleigh knew this was an act as she knew he was very tired and would not be able to continue. And she was right; it was then that she slapped him and gave him the tongue lashing of his life. Their voices were so loud, that Celeste could hear them. Celeste said to Miriam, "well sis, she's blowing her stack; are we prepared to deal with whatever she throws at us?" "Don't worry, we'll be ready for Thing when the time comes."

APRIL 1994

Celeste was returning home from work at the school, when she approached her front door, she noticed that it was open. She entered and looked around carefully as she tiptoed over to the telephone table where she kept a small pistol in its drawer. She opened it to find it gone and then heard the sound of the hammer being cocked from behind her. She turned around to face her attacker but never got the chance to see it as a shot suddenly rang out and tore into her abdomen.

Moments later at her home, Beverleigh chuckled to herself as police and an ambulance raced to Celeste's home. She didn't want Celeste to die yet, as she wanted to frighten her adversary a little. And thought that while Celeste was in the hospital that Everrett would take his mind off Celeste and pay her some attention she well deserved; but she was wrong as his affection for Celeste intensified.

Weeks after the shooting and Celeste was released from the hospital, Everrett was there to accompany her home. He carried her in the house and made her comfortable on her bed. While she rested, he busied himself trying to make her surroundings more accessible as her wounds were not completely healed and she was not able reach for things in high places. As she lay in her bed, Miriam appeared, "Oh this is rich! Everrett Ross Dansfield is doing housework! He never worked like that when I was alive and I gotta say, he damn sure doesn't do this for Beverleigh!" Celeste smirked at this but grew concerned, "Miriam, we've got to make our move soon. I was lucky this time and don't think I can take another hit. We don't need to do anything more, his presence here alone is sufficient enough to make her go over the edge." Miriam thought about it and Celeste was right, their plan was indeed working, but Miriam wanted to change the outcome as the only one to suffer this time would be Beverleigh.

From day to day, Beverleigh watched as her husband went over to Celeste's home to check on her. The woman was gaining her strength back and would be returning to work very soon. Beverleigh was determined to make her return an uneasy one; but first she had to know where this Celeste Holman came from as there were too many coincidences, especially how this mysterious woman was able to worm her way into the Science Lab with Everrett. She had to know or at least find some clues that could prove that Celeste is an impostor as she hadn't the chance to do a thorough search the last time she was there. Celeste had come home just as she was about to look around upstairs; her only find was the gun that was in the drawer of the telephone table. She wondered if Celeste had a motive for using it, or was it just for security? Whatever the reason, Beverleigh was determined to find out exactly what was going on.

JUNE 1994

Beverleigh watched from her bedroom window as Celeste pulled off. This was the break she was waiting for; Celeste had not been going out much since the shooting to give her a chance to snoop. She waited until Celeste was out of sight before going over there and opened the door with a spare key that Celeste gave to Everrett. Miriam appeared and followed her as Beverleigh searched every inch of the first floor and finding nothing. She ventured upstairs and in Celeste's bedroom closet she found a box filled with birth records, copies of adoption papers and newspaper clippings about Miriam's death. Also found was a gun permit issued to Detective Celeste Holman; she was shocked and put everything back in its place as she got out of there ASAP! After all this time, no one had come looking for Miriam's killer until now. Panic set in as there was no where she could go without having Celeste on her trail and now it was vital that Celeste must die.

Later when Celeste returned, Miriam appeared and told her what Beverleigh had done. Celeste's cover was blown and Beverleigh was on the war path, it was time to serve a cold dose of justice to Beverleigh. "Any bets on when she's going to off me?" "Last day of school for staff; she has a flair for the dramatic and will return to the scene of the crime. She has to make sure there's no witnesses, so an empty school building is a perfect place for murder." "But how are we going to let Beverleigh know where I'll be?" "Don't worry, she'll find you! Sneaky ass bitch keeps tabs on everybody. One word of caution, don't keep your back turned around her too long." "Advice duly noted sis." Then Miriam produced a set of rings in a ziplock bag. "It's time we let her have it with both barrels!" "Well in that case, what are we waiting for? Let's do it!"

LAST DAY OF SCHOOL 1994

Celeste and Everrett were in the bathroom finishing their lovemaking while the other staffers were tidying up their rooms and locking them up for the summer. The couple climaxed and lay on the bathroom's cold floor, "Everrett, I think we better finish the lab, it's getting late." said Celeste as Everrett kissed her neck. "It can wait." She pushed him off of her, "I've got papers to run off. I don't want to stay here any later than I have to. Tell you what though, as soon as I'm finished I'll give you the best time of your life." He smiled and replied, "I like the sound of that! Hurry back!" She kissed him passionately as a teaser to what she had planned for him when she returned. She got off the floor and washed quickly in the sink; she felt him watching her and was tempted to rejoin him on the floor but she had to get to the copyroom to deal with Beverleigh. After dressing, Celeste went into the same room where Miriam was murdered; she concealed a small tape recorder on a curtained window sill and went to the closet where she concealed a bullet proof vest.

After all her preparations were done, she then began her charade. It wasn't long before Beverleigh showed up and lunged toward her with a huge blade. Miriam appeared and shouted, "Celeste look out!" Celeste whirled around and threw a stack of papers in Beverleigh's face, knocking her off guard and making her drop the knife. Celeste threw several punches at her face to Miriam's delight and Beverleigh growled like a wild animal as she fought back. She knocked Celeste down with a hard tackle to her mid section, knowing Celeste was still mending from her previous attack. Celeste screamed as she was stunned by the pain and saw Beverleigh reaching for the blade but was unable to move; suddenly, Miriam appeared and said "Don't think so Bitch, you're under arrest." Beverleigh replied as she tried to stab Miriam, "No! You're dead . . . . !! I killed you with my own hands!!" Miriam laughed as Beverleigh passed through her causing Beverleigh to crash into the wall. "Book her Celeste!" "You bet sis." She said as she regained strength to move. Then she retrieved handcuffs from her lab jacket pocket and while Beverleigh was still dazed, Celeste rolled her over and cuffed her. Beverleigh screeched, "You don't have any proof, it's your word against mine!" Celeste replied, "but I do have proof, had a tape recorder going the whole time and I have these." She pulled out of her pocket, the bag containing Miriam's rings and revealed the tape recorder's hiding place. Beverleigh squirmed, "How did you get those!?!" The sisters laughed and said in unison, "how do you think we got 'em?" Then Miriam pat her sister on the back for a job well done and knelt down to look her adversary in the face for the final time. "While you're jail, here's something for you think about . . . Everett still loves me!" Beverleigh screeched, "I hate you both!! And when I get out of here, I'm going to kick both your asses!!" Miriam said, "Oh shut up!" and punched Beverleigh in the face, knocking her out. "Damn, that felt good!!" She said to Celeste, "Well sis, it's time . . . Thanks for everything and kiss Everett for me." Celeste replied, "I'll miss you both too." "What are you saying?" "Miriam, I'm a detective, love and the white picket fence isn't in my job description; I'll tell him everything tonight." "I wish you'd reconsider Sis, if anyone is to be with Everett, it should be you." "I'll think about it, okay?" "Actually, there's nothing to think about; you're two weeks pregnant." "W . . . what did you just say?" Celeste was shocked. "h . . . how do you know?" "I've possessed your body enough to know and that bullet didn't damage anything vital; so go enjoy your white picket fence, and leave the crime fighting to someone else!" She hugged Celeste for the final time and then vanished.

Celeste returned to the lab's bathroom to find Everett asleep and oblivious to all the action that took place. She kissed him; he awakened just as Snow White was by the prince's kiss. "You're done?" he asked groggily. "Not quite," she replied, "I have some confessions to make and a promise to keep. Which do you want first?" He snapped to alertness as he was really curious to find out what the hell she was talking about. "Confessions, then promise." She took a deep breath then told him her true identity and fibbed about Miriam's part in all of this. She said she had stumbled upon the case while searching for her birth parents, only to discover they were deceased and her only sister was recently murdered and felt it was her duty as a detective, and a sibling, to solve the case. Then she told him about the baby. He sat there silently not knowing what to believe for ten minutes; then he got up, dressed and left the lab. She said to herself, "so much for the white picket fence."

On his way out of the building, reporters, and onlookers surrounded him wanting to know the details of Beverleigh's arrest. He wearily replied "No comment" and left them standing there as he got into his car. Angered, that everyone seemed to know what was going on except him, he wanted to get smashed but every bar he visited had a TV and on every channel there was news of what happened. So he went home and drank the bottle of wine he saved for a special occasion. Hours later, his drunken sleep was broken when Miriam shook him awake. He groggily said, "What the hell do you want?" She smiled, "I want you to listen." "leave me alone, I don't feel like having female company right now." She glowered at him, "Get up now, Rett!!" He snapped to alertness as her tone of voice and that God awful nickname seemed to go through him.

After he sobered up and Miriam set him straight, he went over to Celeste's to apologize. She didn't answer the door right away and he worried something happened to her. When she did let him in, the house was in disarray as she was packing it all up for moving. "Hey, where are you going?" he asked. "There's no reason to stay here; the case has been solved and I have to move on." She said as she walked away from him to take down the curtains. He said, "I don't think you should be doing this kind of work in your condition." "What about my condition? You didn't seem to care before, so why the big change now? I won't be in this condition very long, so why don't you go about your business, ok?!" The thought of her aborting his baby unsettled him to talk. So he lifted her into his arms and took her upstairs to her bedroom. She fought him all the way until he dropped her on the bed and when he turned to lock the door, she tried to make her escape out of the window. He grabbed her before she could get the screen out and pinned her against the wall. She threatened, "I'm going to kick your ass for this!" He said, "Listen to me Dammit! I love you and I want you and my child in my life!!" She stopped struggling as his words sunk in. "Oh Everrett, I'm so sorry . . . I love you too but I'm rather new at this commitment thing and didn't think you wanted me after I told you the truth . . ." "Miriam set me straight about everything; fact is, I can't live without you." As they cuddled, Celeste looked over his shoulder to see Miriam sitting on the bed blowing kisses and waving goodbye. Celeste whispered, "thank you" and waved back as Miriam began to vanish; but before her presence exited the room, she whispered, "you're welcome lil sis, I love you."

Suddenly he disengaged from their embrace, "Let's finish packing . . ." She was puzzled, "hmm?" " . . . so you can move into my house!" She laughed at his cleverness and said, "I think the packing can wait; I still have a promise to keep." As they reveled in this moment, he felt light as he was able to finally let go of the memory of Miriam's death and was free from Beverleigh's oppressive spell. A new beginning was dawning for the both of them and as he pulled her closer to him, he initiated that spell that brought them together in the first place.

DEAR DIARY: PASSIONS OF A SEX ADDICT

A widowed husband and his twin college age sons are preparing their deceased mother and wife's possessions for delivery to the neighborhood Salvation Army. While packing, the husband discovers several volumes of journals hidden in an old trunk where she kept her mementos. He stopped packing and decided to read what she had written. As he read, he found most of her writing to be nothing more than insignificant rumblings and gripes about her daily life. He smiled at this, feeling quite secure in knowing that the journals offered no hidden secrets. But unfortunately, his outlook changed after finding two other small books, that were wrapped with bright pink tissue paper. Upon reading one of the little books, he found that it detailed a life that was totally different from what he perceived of his dear, loving wife. The first few pages alone gave way to snatches of a romance with a man named Jamison Demetrii Collier. It began:

Dear Diary:

Although I have several diaries in which I write my inner most thoughts, I reserve this one for the recollections of my memories of Jamison Demetrii Collier, my first love.

We met in the 70's as school children and I beat him up to take his lunch money to buy ice cream. As we grew up so did our friendship and we gave each other the first kiss sitting in the rain. I remember one hot summer night, we went bike riding and broke our 9:00 curfews. We found a dark alley and made out like people possessed! At that time I didn't know it would be the start of something dark and mysterious; there wasn't a time in my life that did not include J.D.C.

1976. He was in trouble with the law and had been sent to the Juvenile Detention's Center many times. It was then that our relationship was really being tested. I was naive and sweet and he often took advantage of that fact. But I didn't mind because as far as I knew I was in love.

1978. We sat on my mom's couch playing with kittens; we get really romantic until we realize one of the kittens had fallen asleep in his jacket pocket. We laugh and think this is really cute and decided this was a sign not to continue our fun. This only stopped him temporarily as he was like a bee to honey and dropped by frequently hoping to get to that final step but I stop him every time as I am not ready to go that far yet.

Late 1978-79. I met several good looking guys in high school and I lost my virginity to one of them. J.D.C. finds out through the grapevine and becomes very jealous and angry. He watches me like a hawk. I can recall, Kevin Morris, who I was sorta interested in at the time came over for a study visit. But I found he was a creep as he tried to trap me in the kitchen and force me into having sex with him. Unfortunately for me, no one was home at the time when all of this was happening, I fought like a wild cat. Suddenly the doorbell rang rescuing me from a fate I consider worse than death. While he was distracted I broke free from his grasp and ran to the door hoping it was a family member who had lost their key or something. To my surprise it was J.D.C. and he was dressed to the nines looking like Superfly! I invited him in and whispered in his ear that I had company and that this company was rude to me. He looked at me and saw how disheveled I looked and he grunted, "I'll take care of him."

Kevin, in the meantime was sitting at the table looking studious and ever so innocent and J.D.C decided to call his bluff. Kevin tried to apply his so-called superior knowledge of the subject we studied, the war of the minds was on! Kevin thought J.D.C. was all "Mr. No Brains" not knowing J.D.C. had an extremely high IQ. This irritated Kevin and he left. It was the best non violent chivalry fight I ever saw.

After Kevin left and J.D.C. helped me with the rest of my homework, we went at it furiously. Months later, he surprised me; as he was leaving for college.

1980. I meet more guys in his absence and was careless. I was pregnant by one of them and I quickly abort it. I feel ashamed of what I have done and sorta "wigged out". I was chain smoking like a sailor and swilling down vodka like it was going out of style. One day I bump into him on the street and he comments that I had gotten really fat. I was reluctant to tell him why, but it didn't matter anyway as he had figured it out and wasn't too happy about it. He kept saying over and over that my body and soul belonged to him. He made it clear that he wanted me to bear his children only; but it went in one ear and came out the other as I would've done the same thing as I am not ready for the responsibility of motherhood. After our chance meeting, he frequently dropped by unannounced while he is home from college. He had become so obsessed with me that in a matter of months, he drops out from college to make sure I'm not fooling around with other guys. He even stops me from destroying myself as with his meddling, I quit smoking and drinking. Things between us heat up alot as we explore other sexual avenues and I like it. Behind his back I see other guys and his suspicious mind flowered. Then I discovered by a fluke, that he had other girls in his life and whenever he ranted and raved about my relationships, I threw it back in his face. One day after a confrontation about this, he made me realize just how strange our relationship really was. I feel cheap but for some odd reason I couldn't explain, I just couldn't get enough of him.

1981. He disappears for awhile only to return to take me to one of his relatives house at which he is staying temporarily. We are alone and get into some heavy petting on living room couch. Suddenly his head was between my legs kissing my eternal abyss. I stopped him because as my conscience got the better of me, as the owner of the house was elderly and trusted him not to disrespect their property.

I don't know what compelled me to stay in this type of relationship knowing that it was purely a sex thing; but the most erotic and romantic experience I endured was at a playground. We we're alone sitting on bench in a darkened corner talking when he decides to kiss me, the next thing I know, he is lifting me onto his lap with me facing him. He makes sure the bottom of my dress is out of the way and opens his fly, brushes himself against me while we get a slow rhythm going. We are almost at the point of no return when he pulls aside the crotch of my panties and enters me hard. I thought I was going to explode! But we were interrupted when some kids came into the playground. The memory stayed with me four days.

1982. Was weird as J.D.C. disappeared again and I seemed to be jumping every Tom, Dick and Harry's bones at the drop of a hat! It got to the point where I would alternate between guys and I never seemed to tire of having sex. By mid year, I hit a dry spell and I was jonesing for male companionship. It was a lonely time but I endured though. It got so bad for me that my brother Steve felt sorry for his dateless sister and set me up with his best friend Chuck. We were going to double date with Steve and his girlfriend Carla. Chuck, was on the rebound just as I was and it didn't take long before we were friends. As a matter of fact, we were instant friends and got a whole lot closer on the ride back home from the date. As Chuck and I sat in the backseat of Steve's car in silence, I felt quite horny! Somehow his hand touched mine and we were soon holding hands and began to kiss. Tender kisses turned into hot, hard kisses that motivated us to give in to the amounting passion. He eased me down on the seat and we made out quietly almost thirty minutes before Steve and Carla realized what was going on. Steve had turned around to say something to us when he discovered us on the seat, "Hey! Break it up you two! I wanted you to like each other, but not that damn much!"

Chuck and I realized that we had nothing in common and that sex was our only link. The only draw back I found being with Chuck was that he was insatiable and his penis was extremely huge before being engorged. Whoever said that size didn't matter ought to be shot! I guess the inventor of the saying had never been stuck together like Chuck and I were once. It was embarrassing as that monstrosity of a penis refused to shrink even after ejaculation and further more, it was painful for the both of us as he tried with all his might to pull out. All we could do was laythere until it decided to dislodge on its own. Believe me, this is one experience I don't ever want to go through again.

July 1982. It was Chuck's birthday and we had made love for the umpteenth time when we were interrupted by a telephone call from his mother who lived in California.Of course she had nothing important to say but he continued to talk to her and by doing so this ended our love fest and I felt spared. I slipped out of bed and went into his bathroom to shower, but no matter how much I scrubbed, his scent was still attached to me. When I left, I bumped into J.D.C. in the street as I was making my way towards home. He kissed and fondled me right in the middle of the street. I told him I was too tired to reciprocate as I had just finished an encounter with someone. He sniffed me and said "he must've been one heck of a guy. His scent is slight but it's still on you." I felt dirty and ashamed and shocked to hear J.D.C. tell me to go home and bathe again and to be ready for him. Despite my tiredness and myself respect, I did as I was told! I took the longest shower in history and when I was done I put on fresh clothing but I decided not to wear any panties. It was a very hot night and I expected it to get even hotter!! He took me back to that playground in the same spot as before. This time we didn't expect any interruptions as it was well past midnight and no child should be out this late. I grew dizzy as he had me on a swing, on the sliding board, on a bench and on the ground; he seemed just as insatiable as Chuck and when he had enough I was quite grateful. As we prepared to leave the playground, he knelt down and nuzzled my crotch. I told him was arousing me again and he replied, "good. I want you to yearn for me, this is just a reminder of is yet to come for tomorrow. Be ready." I didn't like the sound of his voice as it had an evil edge to it and his mood had changed drastically. He stood up and grabbed me by the collar of my dress and very nastily told me be ready or else. I wanted to ask him what I had done wrong but I was so sex drunk that I didn't have the strength to ask; I just followed him out of the playground like a lost puppy.

When we arrived at my door, he pulled me close to him so I could feel him. I pulled away from him and asked, "Don't you think that's enough for one night?" He smirked at me and said, "shouldn't be for a sex fiend like you. But *I* can wait til tomorrow." He gave me a quick peck on the cheek and went on his way, leaving me feeling insulted.

1983. After that insult J.D.C. fed me, I came to the realization that in some way J.D.C. was right. I was a sex addict. And like a true junkie, going cold turkey was painful and miserable but I survived and felt clean.

Nov. 1983. I get a new job and while I was walking home one foggy night, someone called my name. As a matter of fact, the fog was so dense that I couldn't identify who it was until the person was very close. It was J.D.C., as we walked and talked, he seemed so different from what I had known. He was sullen, dark and seemed to be quite on the thin side. I went with him to his apartment and I was shocked to see so much drug trappings laying around in plain view. He sat me down and explained about all the changes he had been through since he lost his job and couldn't find another. He had returned to his old habits as a thief and stick up artist. As for the drug use, he returned to them as well as he hadn't been involved since the days when he was incarcerated at the Juvenile Center. Piece by piece he was breaking down, wanting release from this torment. He sought me out as he knew I was the only person that would stand by him no questions asked. After alot of talking and soul searching on his part, I was able to convince him to give me the drugs and that I loved him very much. I flushed all the packets of cocaine and Quaaludes down the toilet; he stood there in a daze as I did this. I could feel his rage boiling inside and if it weren't for the fear in my eyes I swear if he could he would've torn me from limb to limb. But instead, he allowed me to hold him in my arms for comfort. One thing led to another and I wound up spending the night with him.

December 1983. I visited him on a regular basis, but lately it had been anything but regular. We often talked about how we felt about one another but upon my last visit, he laughed at me and said I was nothing more than a good fuck. I was hurt deeply and refused to let him touch me; he grew angry and was going to hit me until he saw the tears in my eyes. He turned away from me and sat in the corner of the room to smoke a few joints. As he smoked, I was dressing and preparing for a hasty exit. Before he could roll another joint, I grabbed what I could as I knew this was the main reason for the discord in our relationship. I ran out of the apartment and out of the building as fast as I could trying to out distance him while he was still struggling with his clothes. Despite snow and being semi dressed and bare footed, he was hot on my trail. He caught up to me at the street corner as I tried to run across. He caught me by my hair and forced me down in the middle of the street. I recall him saying: "Gimme my shit or I'll fuck your ass up! Don't make me do it!!!" I struggled underneath his weight to gain freedom and when I was close enough to a sewage drain, I dropped most of it into it. He howled like wounded beast, and throttled me, I fought him and told him he had already hurt me and that killing me wouldn't solve his problem. He released me and I threw what drugs I had left in my hand at his face and walked away from him for good.

1984. Or so I thought. We kept running into one another, but we were never quite the same. He was off the drugs, found a job and was now buying a house. We try making a go of it, but failed after a couple of days. Later on that year, I meet my future husband Donald. He is nothing like the men I had previously in my life. He is gentler, kinder, not a drug addict nor is he insatiable or a woman abuser. I am in heaven. We marry and nine months later I give birth to twins. J.D.C. visits me while I am still in the hospital. He passionately kisses me as if I had given birth to his children. When we part, I am stunned and as if on cue, Donald enters the room. The two men greet each amiably but I could feel the tension in the room mounting as the hate and jealousy is revealed in their eyes. Months later, while still on maternity leave, J.D.C. visited me while I recuperated at home. We make love on several occasions, but the passion was gone. I become pregnant again, unsure of who sired it. I quickly abort it and once more I feel ashamed of what I had done. I never told J.D.C. and told Donald that I had to abort it because I wasn't ready to have another baby so soon after the birth of the twins.

1985. Have run into J.D.C. off and on and we both have realize that our relationship as we knew it, is finally over. But still get goosebumps whenever I see or think about him. He still is my one true love despite the misery and bullshit he put me through.

1986. Life with Donald is wonderful as he takes care of his children's and my needs with tenderness, love and responsibility. I try to return his affections with the same velocity; my love and respect for him is deep; but deeper down somewhere I secretly yearn for the passion that J.D.C. has left behind in my soul. My life is satisfying despite this and I wonder if J.D.C, is feeling the same thing I am. Maybe it's best that I never know and keep my secrets locked in these diaries. Donald is special and I wouldn't want to hurt his feelings. I don't want to put him through the misery J.D.C. put me through in the past. Well dear diary, what do you think? Am I one for the lovelorn loony bin? . . . .

There were more entries, but he couldn't bring himself to read them. He closed the book and was angry; how could she have kept such secrets away from him? He loved her regardless of her past and what little details she provided him about it were sketchy but this did not dissuade him from loving her. Although he was aware of J.D.C. as being one of her past lovers, he was not aware that she continued their relationship during their marriage. He thought to himself, "how in the world could she love a bastard like J.D.C.? What kind of power did he have over her to make her so obsessed with him?" But he knew it was no use in getting riled and fired up over it now; she was dead and buried and so were the answers to his questions. One thing was for certain though, if he had found these particular journals before her death, he would have killed her with his bare hands and put her out of her misery sooner than God had planned.

STUBBORN JACK

There once was a stubborn little boy named Jack, who was extremely fond of an old cowboy hat. And every day he would say to himself: "It's plain to see, this hat is perfect for me! And as long as I keep it from out of harm's way, on my head, this hat will stay!"

Jack kept his promise and never took off his hat; everyone pleaded and begged but Jack had made up his mind and that was that.
One bitter cold and windy day, his mother said, "why don't you put on a winter cap for a change; I am sure that your cowboy will blow away."

He said to his mother, "I eat, play and even bathe in it; I even wear it to bed! I like this hat too much for it to ever leave my head!"
He turned with a pout and stormed angrily out to play.

The cold wind chilled Jack to the bone and felt as if he were an ice cream cone. A frosty gust came, blew his perfect hat off his head; he should've listened to his mother and worn that warm winter cap instead.

He watched sadly as the wind carried his hat high into the air, then landed in the highest branches of a tree. Jack tried to shake it down, hoping to set it free, but he stayed out in the winter air too long and caught a nasty cold. As he walked sadly home, something in the back of his mind said, "none of this would've happened if you had done as you were told."

All's well at home now, as Jack said while sipping his tea; "Mother, I apologize, and I promise never again to let anything make a selfish little monster out me!"

SUMPTIN' TO SAY

I GOT SUMPTIN' TO SAY Y'ALL, BUT AIN'T NOBODY PAYIN' ANY ATTENTION. I GET QUIET FOR A MINUTE AND Y'ALL WILL THINK I'M SICK.

SORE THROAT, CAT GOT YOUR TONGUE, MAKE THOSE DUMB STATEMENTS. GO ON 'HEAD, ASK THOSE DUMB QUESTIONS, YOU'LL GET NO ANSWERS.

I TALK LOUD ENOUGH, YET I AIN'T NEVER HEARD. SO IF I "ACCIDENTALLY" LET A CAT OUT OF A BAG, ITS MY GUESS Y'ALL WILL SHUT UP FAST AND THEN HANG ON TO EVERY WORD.

FALL

I fell . . .

        now

              I'm

          falling . . .

                falling . . .

                      into the Pit of Hellfire.

The sin I committed

            was so

                  petty and pretty small.

But break one of God's good rules,

                  you break 'em all!!

        SO,

          REPENT

              REPENT

                  REPENT NOW

          before you take a trip

        and

          fall . . .

              fall . . .

FALL.

THE WORLD IS DOOMED BUT THERE IS HOPE

The World Is DOOMED!

I want to run but I can't hide from this horrible,
sinking feeling I have inside.
The World is doomed!
There's monsters in my room!
Even though it ain't Halloween,
there's an ugly witch outside riding on her broom.

Babies crying dying by parental hands
that couldn't cope; they don't pray to God,
but oh how they worship alcohol and that
ever free flowing dope.

I want to run but where am I to go?
I can't escape this pain lurking in my soul.
Crime running wild . . . OOPS!
There goes another homeless, rejected,
forgotten child . . .
I just wanna escape for awhile . . .
just for a little while.

There's that witch perched on her broom . . .
Look at those monsters in my room . . .
Is it alright now for me to scream?
Or is this all some stupid dream?
A test of faith to see if I can cope
The world's not doomed as long as there is hope.

THE VICTIM'S EYES: A MURDERER'S TALE

He followed her then dragged her screaming and kicking into the shadows of the night. There in the darkness, he tortured, raped her and finally slit her throat. Her brown almond shaped eyes open wide, frozen in time with fright.

No one cared about the crime he committed, but his last victim was going to make sure that he wasn't going to get away with what he had done to her. Ever since that eventful night, every woman he saw had that same frightened stare; no matter how far the distance those almond shaped eyes followed him everywhere. He saw them in his sleep, he saw them in the diner where he would eat. Those eyes were seen in books, magazines and in stores. As time ticked on, he saw them more and more.

He couldn't stand it much longer, but life must go on. "Can't let this thing beat me . . . so boogie man be gone!!" He laughed to himself; it was time to put another murder under his belt. Returning to the scene of his last crime, on a cold winter night; he hid once more in the shadows, waiting for his next victim, ready to strike.

Soon a woman came out of nowhere; she walked stealthfully as a cat sensing its prey's scent in the air. She approached him and faced him with that frightening stare. Recognizing the face, he wanted to run, but he was paralyzed by her eyes. Blinded, he couldn't see what was withdrawn from her coat; a wicked smile smile soon etched across her pallid face. The knife gleamed in the darkness and in a flash—she slit his throat.

The next morning, the police found his body with that same frightening stare; they put his corpse into a body bag and once again, nobody cared. On the wall, scrawled in his blood, his last victim wrote:

DO UNTO OTHERS AS OTHERS DO UNTO THEE: HERE IS THE MURDERING SCUM WHO MURDERED ME . . . .

DYING TIME

Yesterday I saw an awful sight; a man, lying in his own life's fluid reached out to me to help his soul escape Mr. Brink, the Angel Of Death. I was afraid and didn't know what to do; I was about to run and find help when he painfully told me not go. I stood there in a panic as he reached up and held my hand. He quickly told me the story of his life; of how Mr. Brink had stalked him throughout his lifespan, but he kept escaping and Mr. Brink thought the man had become invincible.

He told me that unfateful day, while running from death, he was tricked into a deadly game, where life or death was the consolation prize. But he had lost and death was his prize and I was to become is shield to death so he couldn't be taken away. I asked, "why me? What have I done to deserve death's touch before my time? I just stopped to help a dying man and not to move up my time to die!" He pleaded, "Please stay here, he only wants my soul and he won't touch either of us as long as I don't let you go."

I said, "I know Mr. Brink isn't a fair man nor is he mortal; he doesn't care whose soul he takes, its the less amount and the ones that get away is what he hates. So mister, let go of my hand, a soul is a soul to him and tow souls are better than none; you've served your time in life, give Mr. Brink his due, let go of me and face death like a man, I think its best that you do."

Mr. Brink approached silently from behind and surprised us both and now it was dying time. The man was scared and shaking as a leaf as he lay on the ground, I stood firm in my tracks and didn't make a sound. For I knew I couldn't outrun him because there's no turning back when Mr. Brink comes around.

Mr. Brink, The Angel Of Death, touched his victim, disappeared with his soul and left me intact; never touching touching me as I stood firmly in my tracks. I am no longer afraid of Mr. Brink and accept and expect my time to come as surprise like that day on the street. And I will stand firmly in my tracks for I know for sure that in death, there's no turning back.

CAROL

Once upon a time, there was this girl named Carol whom I met in my junior high school days. Her family, all five of them were sort of weird and had really strange and funny ways.

Carol's sister Mary, was the wackiest and craziest of the brood; she would do a strip tease act in front of the neighbors and run down the street in the nude.

Her mother was the neighborhood whore; whenever any man knocked on her door, she would say with a poor French accent "entree" and they would copulate right there on the floor.

The father liked reading porn mags as his folly and made it with his only son to set off his jolly. The little boy who was only eight years old at that time, thought this was normal and one day while I was on my way to school, I saw him on the street trying to sell himself for a dime.

Carol, seemed to have her head on straight once in awhile, you see, she was a heroin addict and was strung out a mile.

She used to come to school when the lunch bells began to chime and always sat beside me at my table every time.

One day after lunch in the girl's bathroom while she was coming down from a high, she knocked me down on the floor and began feeling my hidden space between my thighs.

I was scared and screamed as I tried fighting her off in that Godforsaken place, she grew angry at my resistance and punched me hard in my face.

The blow broke my nose as the bones shattered with a crack; Carol touching my every part was the last thing I could remember before everything grew black with fear still pumping in my heart.

The next thing I knew as I awoke hours later in a hospital bed, tubes attached to both arms and bandages taped to my face where my nose had broken and bled. While awake, I felt the pains of bruises and whelps everywhere, I was beaten so bad, I had surgery for a ruptured spleen of which i was not aware. I couldn't believe what she had done; how could she be so mean to me, her best and only friend?

A few more hours pass, the police and my mother were asking questions that I wished they didn't ask. I was hurt mentally, emotionally, and physically wanting to desperately cry; my best friend raped and tried to kill me with no apparent reason why.

So I told them everything that had happened through the tears that finally came as my mind was burning and snapping. My mother asked why I never mentioned these things about Carol's family, I told her that Carol needed a friend a I was vowed to secrecy and I was under bound; that was months and years before she hurt me and I was willing to tell all now.

When the police had done their duty, Carol's parents arrested, Carol and her sibling tucked safely in some home, I was glad it was all over now that they were all gone.

That happened in my teen years, now that I am an adult; I sometimes have bad nightmares about it and often think it was all my fault. You see, I found out she was secretly jealous of me because I have my mother's love and care and all the negative things about her family built up in her until she finally snapped and flared.

She always wanted her family to be just like mine but they were all too deep in their own little worlds to care and Carol was deprived.

THE BOYS USED TO LIKE ME

The boys used to like me, that's what they all used to say; They tried to get my attention and prove that they meant it in their own little silly ways. B.G. used to like me, that's what he used to say, then everyday after school, he and his cronies used to beat me up because I refused to look their way.

I used to come home bruised with whelps a-plenty, tears constantly rolling down my face as I walked down those mean streets; naturally I felt ashamed and embarrassed of how messy I looked cause no one, nobody will never imagine how I survived the beatings I usually took.

When I finally reached home and tell my parents all, they got angry and gave the principal a call; he/she said they wanted my parents and me to come up and talk to the other parents too, but the other parents knew that their child was absolutely guilty; show up they never do.

Everyday of my adolescence was spent exactly the same, while I was attending that junior high school. I was never the victor or conqueror, just everybody's punching bag or fool. The boys wanted my affection, attention and they tried to get it in every way; I needed friendship and help and even the girls, they hated me, when asked why they would not say.

One day, when I thought I found a place where I would be safe, B.G. and his boys seemed to appear out of nowhere; the street we were on had nothing but old abandoned buildings, and of course not soul lived there.

Screaming and kicking as they dragged me into an abandoned house, it was dark, scary and dreary and I could feel the presence of the rats readying to pounce. I tried to make my escape through the door, but they were too fast, too powerful and they knocked me down on the floor with a bounce.

B.G ordered his friends to hold me down and to strip me naked, I struggled, was scared and began to cry, a million questions floated through my head, the main one: Why? In the darkness, I heard the distinct sound of someone unzipping his fly.

I screamed and screamed as he came closer, his friends let go of me and B.G. was a-top of me, his manhood burning ablaze. He rammed into my virginal abyss like a knife cutting through cheese. My screaming turned into pleading and begging, "oh please stop, stop it please!" as he ripped me apart, I heard his friends laughing that B.G. has guts and lots of heart.

When he had finished, he kissed me tenderly and wiped away each tear that had fallen so softly. All of a sudden his voice changed from enemy to friend; something was totally amiss. I knew him all too well, he kept kissing me and then he whispered into my ear, "I love you" as soon as he was finished talking, as quick as a flash, he hit me in the face with a brick hoping each breath was my last.

Again the brick came down upon my head, darkness darker than night engulfed me as I slipped into unconsciousness. Angels started to sing, B.G. recovered his thing and he and his cronies left me for dead.

Darkness, darker than the night, when will I awaken to see the glorious light? Darkness surrounding me holding me back from the precious day; and the boys, oh yes the boys used to like me, that's what they meant by saying I love you in their own "special" way.

The boys used to like me in those adolescent days; they tried to kill me and forced me to look their way. I am no longer beautiful to behold, I will never be the same, but as for the boys, to them it was nothing but a silly childhood game.

MIXMATCH

"Shit!!" This can't be! My tubes have been tied for 18 years!" said Chelsea after receiving word from her doctor that she was indeed two months pregnant. Doctor Yoland said, "The procedure can become undone after a certain amount of years, it just so happens this is your time and you're still fertile when most women of your age aren't. So what are you and your husband opting to do, adoption or abortion?" "My husband and I have been divorced for ten years and it's *not* his child . . . this was a total mistake brought on by alcohol and too much partying with friends." Dr. Yoland became concerned, "Did you know him? He didn't force you into this did he?" "No . . . no, it wasn't anything like that . . . the guy has been a good friend of mine for years and I initiated it. The problem is, he's gay." Dr. Yoland raised her eyebrows and looked over her lab reports to recheck the results of the Aids and STD tests. She sighed with relief as all the results were negative, then she started asking questions about Matthew's sexual and medical histories. Chelsea felt insulted and wished she had kept her mouth shut about him; then she told Dr. Yoland she wanted a abortion as the doctor's reaction to this information influenced her decision. Chelsea didn't want another child to raise alone nor put Matthew in a situation he could not handle, and too, she didn't want to be the one to explain to the child that its father was gay. And so Dr. Yoland made the arrangements and everything was set. Afterwards, she wanted to drink herself blind; but despite her plans to abort the baby, a maternal instinct kicked in and she didn't want her alcohol consumption to interfere with the baby's health. So she went to McDonald's instead to have French fries smothered in chocolate milkshake and to mull over whether or not to tell Matthew about this.

It was all for the best she kept telling herself as she recalled how it happened. All the people in their friendship circle were in attendance at the party Jeremy and Matthew gave at their home and alcohol flowed free as if were a river. She was one of the remaining few at the close of the party and Matthew offered to let her stay overnight. She was too bombed out of her mind to walk more or less drive, so Matthew had to carry her upstairs into their spare bedroom. As he laid her down on the bed, she pulled him to her and kissed him passionately and he didn't resist. It must've been the alcohol because normally he would rebuff any attention from the female species; but for that space and time, he allowed her to give him all her affections and one thing led to another and they consummated their burning lust. She remembered the next day being awakened by soft kisses. When they realized what happened, they sprang out of bed, scurried to get dressed as they dared not speak because they weren't sure of Jeremy's location. When they were fully dressed they searched the house for him and found him on the living room floor passed out from drunkenness, oblivious of everything. They went upstairs to talk. "What did you do to me, Matt?" she whispered trying not to to become frantic. "To you!? You mean what did you do to me! Oh God! I haven't slept with a woman for ten years and I was happy with my life! Now you come along and ruin everything!" he said trying not to raise his voice either. "it must've been mighty good to you cause you didn't refuse! So I don't think I ruined you that damned much!!" "Look we gotta stop arguing, this isn't getting us anywhere . . . let's keep this between you and me; what Jeremy doesn't know won't hurt him." "God I feel so dirty and Jeremy's going to feel so betrayed . . . I hope he never finds out" said Chelsea. "Keep your mouth shut and he won't" said Matthew.

And the secret was kept and life went on like clockwork until she began having morning sickness and other pregnancy related ailments. Chelsea wished she could go back to the doctor's office to have that abortion now as she knew her ailments would increase and there was no way she could hide her pregnancy from the world much longer. After leaving McDonald's, she drove around for hours with no true destination to clear her head. It was eleven p.m. when she finally went home and when she walked in, she noticed the answering machine's flash button was winking furiously. Thirty of the thirty-one messages were from Jeremy and Matthew as they were concerned about her health as she was looking more and more fatigued and pale. She felt comforted by their concern and smiled at some of the silly "cheer up" messages they left on the answer machine. She erased their messages and decided to call them in the morning.

It was a beautiful Saturday and Chelsea slept through half of it because even at eight weeks along the fetus was draining all her strength. She would have slept through the rest of the afternoon but she was awakened by the loud ring of her telephone. It was Matthew and Jeremy calling from a pay phone down the street from her apartment building as they felt insulted because she didn't return their calls, so they decided to drop in on her instead. "Be there in a few shakes dollface." said Jeremy then she heard Matthew's voice, "we got something for you that just might put the color back in your cheeks . . . all four of 'em! So cya in a few!" He and Jeremy laughed over his cheeky comment and she mumbled drowsily, "yeah, okay . . . in a few . . ." and they hung up.

She went into the bathroom, freshened up and put on a sweatsuit; before she could find her sneakers or take the rollers out of her hair, the doorbell rang. When she opened the door, they came in with balloons and gifts and giggling like two naughty school girls. "I hate gay guys; they're always so, happy . . ." she uttered under her breath. "Geez Louise! You look like you've been to Hell and back! What happened to you, girl?" said Jeremy. "you don't wanna know." Chelsea said still drowsy and very grumpy. "Aw come on Chel . . . you can tell us. We're you're friends and, you owe us an explanation dear! Your doctor's appointment was at 9 a.m.! So where did you disappear to the rest of the day and why did you diss us? asked Matthew becoming quite concerned. "Matt, Remy, I really can't talk about it now. I don't feel well and I'm tired, so if you're going to cheer me up, do it quick; otherwise, go home." The men looked at each other in disbelief and realized this was serious.

The two men went to hug her and Jeremy asked, "what did the doctor say? Do you have a serious condition? Are you pregnant? What?" With that last statement he made, Chelsea broke down in tears; she promised herself she wouldn't tell Matthew about the baby, the pressure of keeping too many secrets played on her vulnerability and she couldn't deal with it. "I'm soo sorry guys; I can't hide this anymore . . . Matt . . . I'm pregnant . . ." Matthew stepped away from them, "what do mean Chelsea? . . . You can't be, your tubes have been tied for years! I was there when you had it done, remember?!" "Hey! Hey! What's going on here and why are you two discussing this? Hello Remy's in the room!" With that she bawled louder as she really didn't want to say it in front of Jeremy, that the baby was Matthew's. She broke away and locked herself in the bathroom as she couldn't face them. "Go home . . . I'll call you when I get myself together." Jeremy was angry, "I'm not leaving until one of you explains what the hell is going on!" Matthew sighed and listened to her tormented cries; he told Jeremy to sit down. Jeremy did and Matthew held his hands in his and told him the truth. "Let me get this straight, you had sex . . . with . . . her?" asked Jeremy still in shock over what he just heard. "but you're gay . . . . how . . . how could you?" Matthew had tears in his eyes, "we were drunk . . . and neither of us wanted to hurt you, so we kept it quiet . . . now she's carrying my baby. It's like we're being punished for our mistake . . ." Jeremy slapped him, "Punished is right; God don't like ugly girlfriend! That's what you get for cheating on me." Then he left the apartment leaving Matthew feeling rejected and confused.

He listened to her cries for almost two hours then she finally quieted; but did not come out. The silence was deafening and he assumed she fell asleep in the bathtub or something, so he knocked on the door. He knocked for ten minutes and still didn't get a response; this disturbed him, something was wrong, he kicked the door in and found her on the floor unconscious as she had slit her wrists. "No Chelsea No!" he screamed between tears and sobs as he felt his world collapse in on him.

He used her hand towels to make tourniquets to stop the flow of blood and just as he was bringing her out of the bathroom, the phone rang. He put her down on the couch and answered it hoping he could ask the caller for help. It was Jeremy. "Thank God it's you! Remy . . . she tried to kill herself! Call 911! Get help! She's bleeding to death and I've done all I can do . . . !!! "What!?! Alright alright, stay calm—I'm on it and I'll be there shortly ok!?!" "Alright . . ." wept Matthew.

A few minutes later the ambulance arrived and the emt's and the police took over the situation. Jeremy arrived just in time to see the ambulance pull off and so he followed it as he knew Matthew would not leave her side. That's just the way Matt was; no matter the situation, he was always there for a friend and as the thought sunk in, Jeremy forgave them both despite his broken heart. When this was all over, he was determined to make things right with Matthew and if he chose to be with Chelsea and the baby over him, he would respect his choice and be the best friend (and possibly god father to the child) he could ever be.

After she was admitted and her wounds attended to, she rested peacefully in a private room while the lovers discussed their differences outside in the hall. "So what are you going to do Matt? Are you going to marry her and be a father to your child?" asked Jeremy desperate to know the fate of their relationship. "Remy, you know how I feel about you but right now, I'm totally confused, never thought I'd ever be in this type of situation." replied Matthew. "Well whatever you decide, I'll stand by you no matter what." "Do you really mean that? Because I really need you Remy." replied Matt sobbing slightly. "It's all good dude; come on, let's go for a walk." Jeremy said hugging his lover.

The next morning, the lovers returned to the hospital to see Chelsea talking with her gynecologist Dr. Yoland. They didn't enter and listened to their discussion at the door. "I canceled the procedure." said Dr. Yoland as she took Chelsea's blood pressure. "What? I really need this done as soon as possible!" said Chelsea. "I can't move forward if you're going to slit your wrists dear. This proves you're not fit to handle it." said Dr. Yoland. When Matthew and Jeremy heard that, they rushed in and jumped into the conversation. "What abortion? Chelsea, what is this she-quack talking about?" demanded Matt. "Oh shit . . . how long have you two been standing there?" said Chelsea. "Is this the father of the baby?" asked Doctor Yoland. "Yes, he is. That's Matthew and this is Jeremy." "Stop the chitchat and answer the damned question!" yelled Matthew. "Stop hollering at me!! Okay it's true! I made the arrangements Friday when I found out I was pregnant. I thought it was the right thing to do, because I didn't want to break up your relationship with Jeremy.

I wasn't going to tell you anything at first, until you and Jeremy showed up, I blew it as I didn't want to keep anymore secrets . . . ." wept Chelsea. Then Jeremy said, "Chelsea, don't abort the baby . . . I love Matt very much but to go that far and jeopardize yourself like this, isn't right. You know Matt and I have got your back no matter what" Matthew was shocked to hear Jeremy talk like that. Dr. Yoland said, "I'll leave you three to discuss this, because as of this moment, the abortion is canceled indefinitely. Call my office when it has been decided." Matthew said to Jeremy, "Do even know what you've said?" Jeremy replied, "I'm fully aware of what I've said. For years, I've heard you talk about how you wished you could father a child and that not being able to was the only downfall of being a homosexual. I want you to be happy Matt. This has always been your dream, so who am I to keep you from it? It's up to you and Chelsea to make that decision whether or not this baby is to be born." "Thanks but it's up to Chelsea." She couldn't believe her ears, but she said, "it's been 18 years since I've been a mother and I don't know if I have the patience for this sort of thing and I definitely don't want to do this alone." Jeremy said, "We can handle it. Trust me." She said, "And what about your relationship? How is this going to work?" Matthew said, "We'll help financially and care for the baby as much as possible. That's all; nothing will change between us." She gave some more thought to this situation as deep down she really did want another baby but had her tubes tied years ago only because of the bad treatment she got from her husband. "okay, then its settled. I will have this baby." said Chelsea and the two men ran over and hugged her.

The months flew by fast and it was now her time to deliver. She was on her way to the library when the labor pains began; a passerby asked if she was okay and she told him she was in labor. The passerby ran to the nearest phone and soon an ambulance arrived on the scene. After 10 hours of laboring, she delivered eight pounds and 15 ounces worth of a baby boy, and Matthew and Jeremy were overjoyed they had a son. She named him Matthew Jeremy Davidson. The guys were happy about the name and couldn't wait for their new addition to be released from the hospital so they can begin the joy of fatherhood.

Four months passed and the fatherhood joy wore off for Jeremy as jealousy took its place. He watched day after day as Matthew grew closer to Chelsea and he spent less and less time with him. He thought Matthew was taking this father thing too far and wondered if he had slept with her again. He noticed on occasion he would put his arm around her as if she were his mate and kissed her cheek every time she was in his presence. Matthew changed in front of his eyes; he was no longer a gay man and became an average straight family man.

Then one day, while the four of them were returning from the baby's fifth month checkup at the pediatrician's office, he caught the gleam in Matthew's eye and it wasn't for him; it was for Chelsea.

That night as they lay together after sub standard lovemaking on Matthew's part, Jeremy asked Matthew if he was still in love with him. Matthew was shocked and replied, "You know I love you! Why do you ask?" "You made love to me like you wished to be with someone else." said Jeremy. Matthew scoffed, "that's not true, I'm just a little tired, fatherhood is not an easy job you know." "so I've noticed" said Jeremy sarcastically, rolling away from Matthew.

The rift grew wider as days later, Jeremy caught them kissing in the hallway outside of her apartment. They didn't see him but he heard, "This is wrong. We promised nothing like this would happen . . . and what about Jeremy?" Matthew said, "I don't know . . . but I can't help it; I'm in love with you." Then they kissed again and Jeremy left as he couldn't take it anymore.

Days later after that incident, he went to see Chelsea to confront her about what he had seen. Once inside, she made him comfortable like the millions of times she had before as she was always the gracious host. He noticed she was dressed nicely for a change and was cooking dinner; he offered to help in the kitchen, then he noticed the table was set for two, with good china and crystal instead of the usual paper plates and jelly jars and of course, the food were all Matthew's favorites. He tried to remain cool as he watched her go about her tasks, but the more he stared at this scene, jealousy grew to a fever pitch and while she stood at the stove, he grabbed her from behind and grinded himself into her backside. "What's wrong with you? Get off me!" she screamed as she struggled to break free from his grasp. He spun her around and kissed her hard on the mouth and she slapped him. "Get out!! Get out!!!!" He shook his head no, and went to the table and threw the beautiful settings on the floor; and before she could make her escape he grabbed her and smacked her around before throwing her face down on the kitchen table.

He straddled her and said, "I'm going to find out what it is about you that Matthew can't resist." She cried weakly, "Jeremy!!! No . . . !!" She felt him through the roughness of his jeans as he grinded himself into her again then stopped. She thought it was over but he stopped only to lift her dress to remove her panties. Oddly pleased at the sight before him, he unzipped his pants to release himself; with no regard to her, he entered rough. She screamed as he moaned "Oooh . . . yes . . . . You know, sooner or later is what Matt will expect this of you . . . oh yeah . . . . he'll ease you into it . . . . then when you are familiar . . . he'll do it like this . . . ." Her screams grew more shrill as he continued; tired of hearing her cries, he grabbed her by her hair and repeatedly smashed her head into the table, "Shut up!!! You oughta be grateful! I'm preparing you for what's to come . . . ." Thirty laboring minutes passed before he was satisfied and noticed she was unconscious; after withdrawing and dressing himself, he carried her to the couch and laid her down. Looking at the visible damage he caused, he felt remorseful and kissed her swollen lips wishing she would wake up so he could apologize.

Matthew arrived home to find the door unlocked, the smoke alarm blaring and entered the apartment to be blinded by smoke. He ran into the kitchen to tend to the burning cookware and noticed her panties amongst smashed table settings on the floor. "What the fuck—?", he turned to scan further then he saw her, sitting on the couch, staring and rocking back and forth. He sat next to her, and noticed her injuries. "Oh my God! Who did this to you!?" She fell into his arms, and it was then he smelled the familiar scent of sex and Jovan Musk for Men; (Jeremy's brand). "No, he wouldn't . . . he wouldn't dare . . . !!!" Although unable to speak, the look she gave confirmed his worst fear; as he held her closer, he felt a spreading wetness in the back of her dress. "That son of a bitch!!!" he screamed as he lifted her in his arms and carried her to his car. After she was situated, he came back in and got the baby who had slept through it all then drove to the hospital. Chelsea had to be sedated while a rape unit counselor asked Matt a million questions about the attack. Just then Jeremy walked into the emergency room's reception area and the receptionist sent him back to where Chelsea was. She saw him approaching and screamed hysterically. Matthew passed his baby to a nurse; "hold him for a minute" then confronted Jeremy. "You've got some fucking nerve showing up here; I oughta kill you for this!!!" "Pussy whipped father faker, you don't have the balls." goaded Jeremy as he pushed him aside to see Chelsea. "Filthy animal!!" Matthew screamed as he threw the first punch. The security guards broke it up and Jeremy laughed, "So what does that make you? I did her the same way you do me! Face it, you were going to pluke her and you know it! One of these days, that pussy spell will be over and you'll be back to pluking men!" Matthew broke free from the guard that held him and kicked Jeremy's ass. The guards did not interfere as this went on as they felt Jeremy deserved it. He was beaten senseless and that's when the guards broke it up. "Alright dude, he's done, let us do our job." And took Jeremy to the police station.

A year later, Chelsea hadn't spoken a word prompting Matthew to move in to take care of her and Little MJ's needs. But he was weary as she sat in her favorite chair day after day only moving to use the bathroom. After awhile he hired a nurse to come and care for her as this problem increased. His son was walking and talking, seemingly happy but the little one sensed something wrong and Matthew had a hard time trying to ease the boy's worries. All his efforts didn't matter though, she just stared blankly past everyone as she was lost in that realm that the rape locked her mind in. At night, she had no restful sleep as the memory of what happened and of what Jeremy said plagued her; and when Matthew tried to comfort her, she fought him fiercely as she no longer trusted him.

Then one day, after returning from work and picking his son up from day care, he found her gone. He found a note from the nurse that she had left early and had left Chelsea in the house alone. It was only for an hour but in that time frame Chelsea decided to disappear. He frantically called her family, friends and anyone she knew; but was distracted temporarily when he saw his son walk toward the back window as the blinds flapped as the wind blew them. He scooped his son up and put him in his high chair, then went to shut the window. He howled in pain as the sight below tore him apart; she had jumped from this window mere minutes before he arrived.

A month after her funeral, Matthew got a call from Jeremy. He was amiable despite everything. "So, how have you been? They treating you right in prison?" "yeah, everything's cool. Matt, I called to say I'm sorry; she turned you into a real man and I was jealous." "Jeremy, we've always been real men; but I'm the one that should be apologizing; I should've let Chelsea have her way from the start; she knew our arrangement would cause trouble and she was right. We gambled for my dream but in the end, she lost." Just then an operator's voice broke through, "this call will disconnect in two minutes . . ." "damn prison phones, I got two minutes to tell you that I don't expect you to love me or even want to me as a friend anymore, but what I am asking for is your forgiveness." "I forgive you; but like I said, it wasn't totally all your fault. Everytime Chelsea and I went out with the baby, strangers would comment how nice we look together and how great it is to see a man with his family. I wanted to live up to that picture we painted, but I made her promise not to tell you until I was ready. So this makes me guilty too . . . ." Then the operator broke in again, "this call will terminate in twenty seconds . . ." "Keep in touch Matt." pleaded Jeremy "I will. See ya." said Matt. Then they each hung up their receivers and cried as neither man thought their lives would end up like this because of a woman.

A Rude Awakening

I liked him so much! Not that he was so overly good looking nor was he wealthy; but as we worked together, something about him sparked my every emotion whenever I was near him. Then it happened, we were alone, locked in his office supposedly pooling over reports; he made a pass and as one thing led to another, the tender part quickly dissipated. I wanted to stop because I was uncomfortable about some of his actions. But he was relentless and suddenly, I could hear my mother's lectures about the male species running through my ears and consciousness. I kept hearing her voice say, be careful of what you pray for, because you just might get it. Yes, I admit it this was bad. He didn't look like the type to be predator, but there I was, taken like a virgin, and in some sort of glow that isn't a true afterglow. After snapping out of it and rushing to the bathroom to clean up and prepare for the rest of the meeting schedule, I tried not to think about it. As the day went on, I dove into my work and when I was at home I dove into housework.

The next morning I was prepared to tell him how I felt about everything, he surprised me by apologizing and that we should be just friends. I couldn't believe it! I should've lost my temper, I should've ranted and raved and possibly called the cops, but I was just as guilty by wanting him so bad and wishing he make love to me. And so he did, and now it was over; just like that. Never again will I ever let my crushes over rule my sensibilities and the next time I fall for a man, I will let my mother's warnings engulf me and hopefully save me from the same grievous error.

Be Careful Of Whom You Kiss

Be careful of whom you kiss
for this person may host a dagger hidden in the mist.
For each stolen moment tasted and memorialized
remember it well for such a theft sits not well In God's eyes.
Be careful of whom you kiss
when enuendo and lustful talk becomes a reality
look before you leap or else you'll be facing a life of uncertainty
Be careful of whom you kiss
when the entities that rest between your lap
does your thinking and awakes from its nap
you'll find yourself in a place that you can't
escape with just a slap in the face
Though your eyes may like what they see
and your heart may say he's the one
But where will you be, after its all said and done?
The touch, the feel, the reactions and sound
One rule you shouldn't dis,
a sigh is a sigh and love is just what it is
But before you begin, you must remember this,
Always Always, Be careful of whom you kiss.

RUB A DUB DUB

Oh here I am just your average single woman with nothing better to do with my time than to sit in my bathtub and and fantasize about this guy I am in love with. He however, doesn't even know I am alive and the most he's ever said to me was a mumbled grunt.

In the heat and calmness of the hot water, I drift upon my bath pillow soaking in luxuriously scented water, with rose petals floating serenely throughout . . . suddenly the bathroom door opens and there is a gush of cool air coming from the hallway. Then he is there standing in the doorway with a bouquet of wild flowers and more roses; their fragrance over powering the concoction that already fills my bath and the room itself. I gasp with a shock and try to cover any part of me that is exposed, too shocked for words, I say nothing. He stealthily approaches, with his steely brown eyes smoldering and sparkling, telling me silently, just how much he loves me too. Then he places the flowers in a vase that I keep on the toilet tank; puts the lid down and rests himself, still staring at me and me staring back. The silence is unnerving, so I ask; "why are you here?" He smiles broadly, showing his perfect white teeth and how sexy his mouth is, he says, "Isn't this what you want?" I smile sheepishly and say, "yes I want you . . . I love you." "then what is the problem?" he asks. I say, "only in fantasy do you ever notice me . . . in real life you pass me by." He considered what I said, "in real life, I may be a creep but here I am not and I am here to fulfill your every dream. Please, let's not dwell in reality and enjoy this moment we have." He leans in and kisses me so passionately, I think I fainted . . . I was drifting and floating as his lips were tender and sweet. Even though fully clothed, he joins me in the tub and the passion is in full swing. But after his clothes come off and we get quite busy, I wake up.

A man in a uniform of some sort is standing over me . . . . and so is my roommate and a few policemen. I am still in my bathroom, but I feel the coolness of the tiled bathroom floor and that sexy man I fantasized about is gone. I had slipped on those darned rose petals in my bath water when I was getting in and hit my head on the rim of the tub; my roommate came in just in the nick of time as I had been submerged in the water for quite awhile and was drowning. But Damn! Its shame I'll have to guess how the beautiful dream ended, cause after this accident, no more fantasies and I'll be taking showers from now on.

THE FINDING PLACE

Now for the first time in over a century, the United States is at war on its own shores. Bloodshed is a constant, but yet, love reigns supreme, loyalty and friendship abounds and courage and faith is strengthened through it all.

It started with the 911 bombings of 2000 and everyone was in an uproar over Bin Laden and the war on terrorism was borne. When all the media died down about it, afterwards came the war about Saddam's nuclear threat and all of America was on alert at all times for any type of attack to come. As we Americans were sidetracked by this new war effort, all the terrorist groups with peeves against America and who were disgruntled with our efforts to eradicate them, decided to pool their resources together to take us out and to keep us out of their business. America, the big number one is not so big anymore as now we're paying the price for our open door policies and peace keeping efforts.

Our enemies have occupied major sections of the country, and our once glorious land of opportunity now looks like some of the WW2 pictures I've seen in history books. Immigrants who used to risk their lives for the American dream now dream of somewhere else as the land of milk and honey, has now dried up. Millions of people are homeless, and those most fortunate to live in untouched areas are now the promise lands and shelters of those who survive the attacks. Pennsylvania and New Jersey are strongholds and we citizens are living under marital laws. We eat, sleep and shit when they tell us to and are allowed to work certain places and times. However, despite these conditions, it is worse for those of Jewish or

Israeli descent as some terrorist bands are hunting them for sport. The group that has occupied Philadelphia are mostly Palestinian rebels and they are copying Hitler's atrocities to make a statement against Israel and are using American Jews to rub salt in an already festering wound.

I used to live in Center City, which is located in the business section of the city, but it is now occupied by a faction of the the terrorists who have the nerve to call themselves, The Rambos. I was forced out of my home and shipped to a run down house in a South Philadelphia slum, where they are relocating only women and children. Our food, water and other necessities are rationed and we live like slaves as we are under heavy guard and no one is allowed to be on the street after 11 p.m without a pass. Deplorable living conditions is the norm as for each two or three story row house, as many as twenty four people fight for space. I however, was unfortunate to find a space in the basement of the house I am assigned to. Despite the luxury of having this tiny space, I hate basements! I can't stand the feeling that I am in a crypt and what makes matters worse are the critters that thrive in them! I shouldn't complain though as I could've suffered the fate of my siblings as they were executed. I guess I was lucky as I was just shipped off along with fifty other women to this stinking women's holding center. Despite my mood and hate of all this, I hope nothing has happened to my mom, I've haven't heard anything about these bastards taking over the section of town where she lives. Lucky for her, she lives in the outermost burbs, and most of those sections haven't been touched as of yet. She is the only relative I have now and I pray that when this war is over, and I survive, I don't want to be in this world without family.

Its dinnertime, and I don't know what to expect as rations are few. It used to be what's left over from the night before but those days are gone as some of the women here are pregnant and they get more than us non preggers. Tonight, its stew but I've lost my appetite and gave it to Nia, who is six months pregnant and I went back to my little corner of the basement to sleep.

At five a.m., I am awakened by a centipede crawling on my leg. I screamed as I knocked it off and was really shaken by this but I was more afraid I alerted the guards that patrolled outside. I got myself together and decided I had to get out of there. So I stole through the house and out the front door, the guards that patrol the street had just passed and I quickly darted across the street where an abandoned house stood. It was in such bad shape that even the Rambos refused to use it, but I was willing to take my chances. I hoisted myself up on a broken front window sill and was about to slip through the broken panes when suddenly a spotlight shined on me and two guards ordered me to stop. Wanting to live, I surrendered peacefully and they took me back to my assigned house and made sure the door was locked and guarded well this time. As I sat in my little corner of the basement, squashing every bug I saw crawling in the dawn's early light that came through those dirty basement windows; I became even more depressed. At seven a.m., I cleaned myself and laundered the dress and underclothes I was wearing and put on the only other pair of clothing we are allowed to have. I hurried through my grooming rituals as I had to be ready in time for the pick up truck that takes workers to the metal plant at 7:45. Even though some of us are forced to work at these metal plants, I am glad to go because it gives me eight to eleven hours away from the hell hole which is the South Philadelphia Women's Holding Center. It also gives me a chance to be with friends who are held captive too, but are in holding centers spread out across the city.

My best friend is Samuel Sands and we've been friends for ten years. Sam is Jewish and is masquerading as another nationality as all of the captured Jews are. In spite of our forced labor, and the the risk of being caught doing so, we manage to make each other laugh as our silliness helps us forget where we are. Not only is frivolity of any kind not allowed, talking is too and if anyone must use the bathroom, we must raise our hands like school kids and wait to be recognized before being dismissed under guard. Right now, I have to go so bad, and I know they're ignoring me on purpose as they like torturing us by making us wait and causing our guts to burst. After fifteen minutes of raising my hand, I am finally recognized and I smuggle a pencil in my pocket as I saw another good friend of mine as she also was being allowed to go to the bathroom. A note written on toilet paper, came through the spaces between the stalls. "How's UR relat w/ Sam?" I almost laughed aloud, but caught myself and wrote back, "just friends." Another piece came through, "Yea right!" As I flushed my waste and the notes, a guard rapped on the door signaling time was up. Despite the watchful eyes of the guards, I smiled to myself over the fact that people thought Sam and I were an item. Wrong place, wrong time but a nice thought though. However, my lovely thoughts faded as I got back to my place on the line, a flurry of activity was going on and Sam and I looked at each other with worry on our faces. A guard caught our exchange and told us to keep our eyes on our task and not to talk. Even though we were not allowed to look, there was a woman screaming and alot of scuffling and we knew that another innocent was to be executed. I tried to stifle sobs as tears rolled down my face as I recognized the voice of the woman being taken away and realized another one of my friends was going to die. Sam, despite not being able look at or touch me, knew I was breaking down and began to hum a song. Despite all the noise of the machines and surrounding activity, his voice was loud enough for me to hear and I let it sink in and soothe me until I cried no more. Good ol' Sam, no matter the situation, he always knows what to do to make me feel better.

The nine p.m. whistle blew and our shift was over but damn; Sam and I were detained as we were leaving to go to our assigned trucks. We were arrested because somehow they were informed that Sam was Jewish. They took us to a nearby police station that they overtook and locked us in a cell. We clung to each other for strength as we thought we'd never see daylight again. A guard appeared outside of our tiny cell and stuck his rifle through the bars to put the gun to Sam's head. Sam closed his eyes in expectation of a gunshot but it never came. The guard snickered at Sam's reaction then moved the gun from him and pointed it at my crotch. He rubbed it with the gun and I felt like retching but I didn't want my enemy to know how intimidated I felt. My anger grew as I can't believe this piece of shit wants to fuck me! Sam assessed the situation and winked at me, as if to say go ahead, do him. If this were a different time and place I'd smack him for such a suggestion but I was sure he had a plan of action in mind. So I closed my eyes and like the good actress that I can be, I pretended I enjoyed it. That brute took the rifle away and called for me to come near the gate of the cell and opened his fly for me to do something with his inflamed member. As I reluctantly handled his manhood, stomach acid rose in my throat but I swallowed it as I didn't want this piece of shit to see through my act. I was very convincing as he glared at me as if I were a two bit whore; I didn't know how much longer I could stand to do this and I wished Sam would hurry up with his plan, if there was one. Needing air to quell my sickness, I stepped away and opened my blouse so he could get a good look at my breasts and I said in my best Marilyn Monroe imitation, "come and get me, big boy."

Hypnotized, he opened the cell but used the gun to move Sam away to approach me, that's when Sam ripped the sheet off the bed and wrapped it around the man's throat. Although the man thrashed about, Sam refused to let go. Within minutes, the man dropped the rifle as his strength waned and soon it was over. Sam took the rifle, the keys and the man's belt and we ran out of there.

Along the way of our escape, using our newly gained resources, we tackled many of the enemy and freed our fellow captives. Unfortunately, our escape to the street was thwarted as we were overtaken by more guards than we could handle. Recaptured, we got sent to Holmesburg prison which was now used as a death camp. We held hands during the trip, as a secret message that meant no matter what, our bond was unbreakable. After arriving there, despite Sam's objections, our fellow escapees attempted a small revolt but were quickly mowed down by rifle fire; we didn't participate in it and so we were alone. Sensing an interrogation was next, Sam whispered, "we must survive, so put on the best performance of your life and pretend you are my wife. You are Naomi-Chantel Sands." Naomi is his wife's name and so's not to confuse me and I could stay in character, he combined both our names. His hunch was correct and they separated us for a brief time to grill us on our identities and accused us of being members of the Jewish Underground. They asked alot of personal questions about Naomi and her family and I thank God, that I knew enough about them to pass this test. But when they asked about the Jewish Underground, I panicked as I didn't know what they were talking about and told them so. About an hour after the inquisition began, one of the interrogators reported to his superiors that Sam's answers mirrored mine. They weren't convinced about our information, but they didn't harm us either and still allowed us to be together. Even though we were glad for this tiny act of humanity, we were curious as to why, as these terrorists were well known for their viciousness and lust for blood. They taunted us off and on but still they didn't do any real physical damage and we kept our cool as we didn't want to show them any weakness to provoke them to kill us.

Hours later as we huddle on the metal bed in our new cell, I feel comforted by his warmth. He kisses me on the head and said, "you did good kid." I tried to contain my tears as this whole thing rattled me, and I offered a weak "Thank you." Nestled against his chest, I let my tears fall freely and he said with a confidence I didn't have, "don't worry, everything will be alright; just stay strong and remember what I told you." I wish I could believe that things were going to be okay as he said, but things didn't add up and I wanted to know what those sons of bitches were planning for us.

However, our answer came in the morning, as we were taken to the infirmary and stripped of clothing. I've never seen Sam naked before, and it was extremely hard not to react over this sexy sight; however, he never saw me naked either but he didn't react at all, this hurt my ego somewhat but when I looked at his steely brown eyes, I saw that he was plotting something. Well anyways, what appeared to be an Iraqi doctor gave us physical examinations and we felt violated as his nasty little hands explored every nook and cranny of our bodies and took samples of our bodily fluids.

As this man gave me a pelvic exam, I wanted to cry as each touch brought misery. Sam kept encouraging me to stay strong but our captors shut him up by hitting him with a butt of a rifle. Upon the approval of the doctor, two guards made us sit on a hospital bed together then they pushed us around with their rifles to manipulate us to have sex. We reluctantly surrendered and my nervousness nearly gave away our plan of us being married; but Sam was quick and kissed me passionately to make the act convincing. Oh how I've dreamed to be in the arms of the man I secretly and truly love and to be made love to so passionately that it can't be described; but because of our situation, all the happiness of this dream faded. Sensing my fear, he sweetly whispered, "I don't want to do this either, but our lives depend on this charade." "I can't . . . not with them watching." I said trying to stifle sobs. He nibbled at my neck, he whispered, "just pretend you are at our house and we are role playing in our lovely brass bed, *Naomi*." I looked into his pleading eyes and understood his suggestion; I let my mind wander into my usual fantasies about him and began to relax. As we continued, I noticed his passion was more sincere and I realized, there was a mutual love under the lies. They watched us intensely as if we were actors in a porn movie and Sam saw my disgust in my tears. When we finished, we were pulled apart and the doctor collected our secretions for further study. He waved his hands and they took us out of that wretched place with Sam and I fighting them every inch of the way as without the doctor's protection, the guards groped us.

They stopped once we were met by a ranking officer and they saluted him. He inspected us like we were cattle and when he came to me he kissed me harshly. I fought him and Sam jumped into the frey but was stopped by the other guards. They carried Sam away at the ranking officers insistence and he dragged me screaming and kicking into his office. He said in perfect English; "I love having female prisoners, especially beautiful ones like you!" I smacked him and he punched me in my face and knocked me down. Before I could recover he was on top of me, pinning me down on the floor, "that wasn't very nice. Now I have to be mean." He said as he undid his pants and was about to enter me when there came a knock at the door. He redressed and went to it. The messenger was frantic and even though I couldn't identify the language spoken, I could tell something was happening elsewhere in the prison that needed his attention. He called for several soldiers, gave them orders regarding me and then he left; then the soldiers dragged me into a room where they turned on huge water hoses to clean me and afterwards, I was given an orange prison jumpsuit and sneakers to wear and taken to another section of the prison. The seclusion of this section gave me the impression that I could easily die here and no one would know until the war was over. Moments later, Sam was thrown in the cell looking no better than I was as he too was beaten and threatened.

We embraced and I shivered in his arms as torturous sounds bounced off the walls, and yet, he remained aloof as if nothing was wrong. My suspicion of him being part of some evil plot disturbed me and later, as I paced like a caged animal, I was about to ask him about his attitude, when he smiled at me and told me how cute I look when I'm upset. I asked, "What's wrong with you? How can you sit there and say something like that? We're prisoners and God knows what else they're going to do to us!" His smile waned as he replied, "Sweetie, I refuse to give them the satisfaction of seeing me squirm; it doesn't look like we're going anywhere anytime soon, so sit down and relax." That sounded so cold and despite our ten years of friendship, I now felt like I was in the presence of a stranger. Sam always maintained a free spirited, even tempered and fun outlook; never in my wildest dreams did I suspect that he was capable of murder or the ruthlessness that he is now displaying. I'm scared.

As darkness befell this cold Godforsaken place, we shared the tiny bed in our cell and listened to the sounds of torture echoing through the empty halls. Again his warmth and the gentle beating of his heart comforted me, but as the sounds grew more intense, and despite my newly mixed feelings about him, I could no longer maintain my cool and I sobbed uncontrollably. He felt my body jerking underneath him and began to sing to quiet my tortured spirit. Like a child, I buried my head deeper into his shoulder; he lifted my head up and kissed me and I savored those soft lips that seemed to touch my very soul. Suddenly, a bomb blast shook the building and we held each other tighter. I felt Sam's heartbeat race and I realized he was just as scared and confused as I was and it was his drive for survival that made him do the things he had done to keep us alive. My mistrust vanished and I found myself wanting to stay in his embrace as I desired him more than ever.

Damn, Chantel looks so sexy when she sleeps; but our embrace is adding to the mixed feelings I have as I've always fantasized what it would be like to make love to her. I've never acted upon these feelings because of Naomi and my own insecurities. Now I know that I should've done so sooner, but its a shame that something that should be intimate and full of love between two people, could be so ugly and tragic. Why did they make do that to her? I was disgusted by this act at first, but then my perspective changed when I convinced myself that I was doing this for the good of JU and keeping us alive. But all that went out the window the moment she gave in to the fantasy I subjected her to. Passion took over the both of us and then the act wasn't so brutish as our feelings for each other are mutual; its just a damn shame that an act of rape had to be committed in order to find the truth.

I fear she'll never forgive me regardless of the circumstances that brought us to this. I want her in my life and I vow that I will do everything in power to keep her safe. There is more to her than just a pretty smile and a bodacious body, she is a fighter and a team player. She really held her own during that skirmish and she saved my life several times over; she is totally amazing. She'd make a good soldier for JU . . . Sam dropped that last thought as it was JU that had lured Naomi away from him. As Naomi climbed higher up the ranks, she became more of a soldier than a wife to him and he was miserable. Watching Chantel sleep, he dismissed that thought of her becoming a soldier, as he didn't want the same thing to happen to his relationship with her. He wanted to think about other things but the sandman claimed him and he soon drifted off to a dreamless sleep.

"ARRRGGGGHHHHH!!!!!!" screamed Neil Horlbeck as the leader of the terrorist group that controlled Holmesburg prison, snuffed a burning cigarette into the palm of his right hand. "who is the leader of the Jewish Underground?!" demanded the commander. "I . . . I . . . don't . . . know . . . I swear, I don't know!!!!" whimpered Neil. "You are Jew, are you not?" Asked the commander. Neil replied as tears of pain trickled down his face, "Yes . . . yes . . . I am a Jew and I'm *proud of it!*" "Proud enough to die for your belief, hmm?" said the commander as he withdrew a huge dagger from the top drawer of his desk. He motioned with his head for two of the guards in the room to restrain Neil. "I am a patient man and I like to watch as my victims die slowly and painfully . . ." said the commander as he carefully cut open Neil's shirt and nicked his left nipple with the tip of the blade. Neil winced and tried not to scream but he couldn't hold back when the commander made a deeper cut on his abdomen. "I'll talk!!! I'll talk!!!" he screamed. The commander smiled, "that wasn't so bad was it?"

Days later, our captors brought another man to our cell; he was badly scarred and beaten and we went to help him after they threw him down on the floor. It was then that we recognized he was Sam's friend, Neil. We assumed, just like us, one of those spies had ratted him out and he was sent here to serve out his sentence. However, as we helped Neil to our only bed, I noticed he was wearing a very expensive watch; no prisoner is allowed such a luxury and I began to suspect that Neil was here for another purpose. I waited until Neil was asleep before I told Sam what I suspected, but he was angry at me for my accusation and replied as he shook me, "How can you say such a thing? He's like a brother to me, and he'd never betray us like that!" Once more I found myself afraid of him as despite witnessing the killing of that guard, I've never seen him angry. I said despite risking another jolt, "How can you be so sure?" His angry brown eyes blazed and then he turned away, and I stood there shivering again and knowing not to cross him ever.

A week passed with the three of us taking turns using the bed, sharing the few rations and using the bed's only sheet as a curtain whenever I bathed at the sink or using the toilet. I don't trust that Neil; I remember when we first met at Sam's engagement party, he made a lewd pass and I slapped him. We tussled and Sam came to my rescue; then Neil said these stinging words: "She's a fucking hoochie and I treated her as such!" How ironic he said such a thing since my outfit was extremely conservative compared to what some of the other female guest's wore; however, because I am well endowed in the right places, it just fit *nice* and this was the reason Neil and the other men at this party took notice of me. Meanwhile, Sam had taken Neil to the backyard to talk to him while the other guests tried to calm themselves and reassured me that I was welcomed. Neil was sent packing and the party went on. But this time, there's no party and Neil can't be ejected; I pray that Sam remembers this and knows that there's no chance in hell I'll ever trust Neil.

Two months passed and our captors still watch us like research animals in a lab. They continue to force Sam and I to copulate despite Neil's presence and examine us every other day. Neil contently watches us as it is obvious he wants to be in Sam's place and knowing how sneaky he can be, I don't know who to fear more, our enemies or him. Then it happened, I conceived and our captors were pleased and so is Sam as being a father is his dream but I could see it in his eyes, that he wished I truly were Naomi. I wish this was happening to Naomi too, because it's not my desire to have children and now I am forced into motherhood and being a prisoner of war. As much as I love Sam, we stand on opposite sides of the baby issue as he says that its every woman's job to have children and to populate the world. How chauvinistic and sexist of him; but this doesn't deter me from my conviction; I'm just not the mothering type and don't want any children not even his! I didn't hide my feelings and we argued bitterly just like an old married couple and the guards outside our cell thought our tiff interesting enough to be a soap opera scene. Then Neil came over and said something that chilled us to our bones; "Knock it off you two! Fighting over this won't solve anything because the moment that baby is born, they'll take it and you'll never see it again. So you'll have your wish, *Naomi.*" He laid on the bed and tried to sleep while we stood there with our mouths open, still in shock. Sam roused him and asked how he knew that. Neil told us he witnessed a baby snatching while he was assigned to another cell before he was sent to us. Sam demanded, "What do they want with the babies? What can we do to stop this?" Neil replied dryly "Don't know, nothing and I don't care." Despite this terrible information and my aversion to it, I still don't want this child; truth is, not only is it an out of wedlock baby, its also a rape baby. Regardless of how Sam and I feel about each other, he was forced to do it and our charade only helped make the deed easier for the both of us. This baby is what is it and maybe its best that our captors take it but I would feel guilty if it were harmed in some horrible way. In my heart, I want this child to be with people who would raise it properly and love it unconditionally; unfortunately I am not that person and if this unforgivable act comes to pass, then that is what I wish the outcome to be. God I am so weary thinking about it as this situation is a giant pull on my emotions; however, the good things to come out of this pregnancy is that rations have been increased, our captors are less abusive and I am closer to Sam.

Time is moving slowly and my belly is getting bigger. Sam still harps on the so-called, "wonderfulness and importance" of motherhood and I still defend my reasoning and denials. However, I am haunted by thoughts of the horrors the Nazi's committed upon Jewish children and I wondered if this was what the Rambos plan to do too. These ponderings caused me to have crying jags and both men couldn't, wouldn't or didn't understand my inner conflict and mistook my emotional outbreaks for pregnancy related mood swings. I hate it when the men concur with each other as it makes me feel so isolated for being a member of the "male labeled" weaker sex. I let them have their fun; and even though I hate being knocked up, I don't want the Rambos trying to oblige me by giving me an abortion. When baby arrives, I will fight to the death, with or without the men's help, to insure that baby will live to enjoy freedom as every American should.

During my fifth month, my mood shifted and with Sam's help I came to embrace my impending motherhood. He has been very attentive and the script that we have acted for our captors benefit was now gone. Everything we do is like second nature to us as if we truly were meant to be. I've searched for this kind of love all my life and now I've found my place in the universe. It's a shame that such beautiful sentiments has to be carried out in this time and place. The other thing that bursts this lovely bubble is Neil as he reminds me of a vulture, as he's always lurking around and waiting to pounce. He doesn't talk to us too often and he always has a shifty look about him which makes me uncomfortable. I want to tell Sam, but I don't want to feel his wrath again nor do I want to disturb the domestic harmony we now share; so I keep my mouth shut and hope the truth would surface without my aid.

Time ticked on and so did life as at sixth months, my cellmates were taken away and I was given a mattress, linens and pillows to make that metal bed comfortable and they no longer pointed rifles at me to do anything as they observed my movements. But they constantly make light of my swollen belly and breasts as the orange jumpsuit isn't fitting anymore. So I took it off, and the guards cheered as if I were a pregnant stripper. Then I used some of those linens to drape myself in bedsheet sari's but as soon as I wrapped my head like the women of their country, they stopped their folly and turned their backs to me and I spent the rest of my time in peace.

The seasons changed and the moments alone gave me a chance to reflect on my relationship with Sam; I don't know if this is the pregnancy talking or not, but I like being the love of his life and am tired of being a mistress, and an impostor. I am Chantel Jones and Naomi-Chantel Sands does not exist! I'm afraid that when this war is over, and Sam reunites with Naomi, I'm going to be forgotten and alone.

Again my timing is bad as months before he met Naomi, I told him how I felt about him and he rejected me, stating that he liked me only as a friend. Actions speak louder than words, as it was his constant promiscuity that led me to my assumptions but he was too afraid to take our relationship to that level because of our cultural differences. I don't say this to make excuses for him but all the signs were evident as whenever we were out alone, other people in our vicinity thought we were dating or married. That was then and now I want him to remain being enamored with me, once our baby is born and beyond. But again, I'm grasping at straws, as this is the charming, heroic, steadfast, and married Mr. Samuel "Lancealot" Sands we are talking about.

In this last trimester of my pregnancy, The Rambo's have provided me with more rations and books to entertain me and also more sheets so I can use them for dresses as I can no longer wear the jumpsuits. But despite all these comforts, Oh, I feel so miserable . . . . the baby is due any minute and it is so hot in here . . . and I wish Sam were here to see me through this. Seeing how miserable I am, one of those Rambo bastards tried to upset me further by telling me details of the rape of a pregnant woman he committed, I threw a pillow at him and told him to shut up and I continued to think of Sam. Despite my despair, I thought of the tortures he might endure wherever he was, so I prayed more than ever for his safety. Despite being a Christian and believing that in times of need, everyone should be included in a prayer, however, I didn't feel that way about Neil.

In another part of the prison where five or more men are housed per cell, Neil watched Sam pace the floor. It was midnight and in the bedless cell, the others found places on the floor to sleep. Sam carefully stepped over them as he paced and Neil could see that his friend was in very much need of sleep. Neil left his corner and went to him; "Sam, why don't you catch some z's." Sam replied, "I can't Neil, I'm worried about Naomi." Neil said slyly, "which one, Sam?" Sam cast a tired eye at him, "both of them." Now that Sam seemed vulnerable, Neil saw the perfect chance to grill him about the Jewish Underground and its "Unknown Fearless Leader" But he decided to ease in to it by asking about Chantel. "You know, I've been meaning to ask you Sam . . . how come you told the Rambos that Chantel was your wife?" "I have my reasons and I'm glad you kept your mouth shut." Sam replied wearily. Neil sneered in the darkness, "Was it because it was the only way you could get into her panties?" Angered, Sam grabbed Neil by his throat, "You disgust me right now, so I advise you to quit the inquisition." He released him and Neil slunk back to his corner rubbing his throat. "I was just stating the obvious! You've been sniffing around that bitch ever since you met her. So why don't you admit it, you've always had a deep rooted chocolate fantasy and you really do wish she was your wife." Too tired to dignify that with an answer or to throttle him again, Sam replied, "shut up and go to sleep!" He had forgotten how uncouth and cold his friend could be and didn't need to have his feelings scrutinized right now. Even though he considered Neil his lifelong friend, Sam didn't always agree with Neil's attitude or actions. He was crude at the wrong times and seemed to always say the wrong thing to women which inspired Sam and Josh to take him in as a "pet project" to improve his etiquette and self esteem. No matter how rude Neil was, he was loyal to Sam and Josh and the three of them acted more like brothers than friends.There was a long pause of silence between them and then Neil settled in his corner while Sam went back to his pacing and stepping over the other sleeping prisoners. Neil realized getting the necessary information out of Sam tonight wasn't going to happen, so he gave in to the sandman's calling, and closed his eyes to sleep.

Sam felt he were losing control of himself as the night sounds within the prison depressed him further. He thought over everything he had done since his captivity, hoping that his efforts gave his wife, the true Naomi Sands more time to find safety. The night the large band of Rambo forces raided the Jewish Underground meeting he and Naomi hosted, Sam and other JU soldiers acted as decoys to allow Naomi and other principal figures to escape through hidden tunnels under the floor in the basement. Captured and taken to a men's determent camp in North Philadelphia, he was sent to work at the Metal plant where he encountered Chantel. He was never so happy to see a friendly face as he didn't have many friends left. When he was reunited with Chantel at the plant, he vowed he would do his best to keep them both safe and her close to him as her presence at the plant helped make the time pass quickly and the surroundings didn't seem so bleak. Even though he loved her and she was now having his baby, he felt regretful of how this event came to be. Yes, he wanted this baby, but the fact that he was forced to commit rape upon one of his best friends hurt him deeply. "I hope she forgives me for what I've done" he said quietly. Then he thought of the Rambos's actions to date and suspected they knew Chantel's identity; but was curious, as to why they were given the soft treatment instead of the sadistic tortures the Rambos were known for. Sam suspected that this had to be orgistrated by someone else but who could it be? At that thought, he yawned as sleep claimed him and he curled up in a vacant corner of the cell and put all his worries, regrets and plans to bed.

The next day, he awoke to find Neil missing. Then around 10 a.m., three of the other prisoners sharing the cell were taken out in the corridor and shot to death. Sam and the remaining two stood there in shock after witnessing such a horrorific scene. One of the men whimpered as he cracked, the other tried to comfort his friend and began to cry himself as he feared they were next. Sam didn't move from where he stood as he felt numb and emotionless; then suddenly the world began to spin and the room grew dark as Sam blacked out.

Meanwhile, in the Rambo's command center, the Commandant threatened Neil. "Please!! Just one more chance, he's ready to crack!" he cried after being smacked around. "And why should I believe you? You've had more than enough time to get the information and here you are with nothing! I'm usually a patient man Mr. Horlbeck but you've put me in a terrible position . . ." said the Commandant as he stood behind Neil and cocked his revolver close to Neil's ear as he squirmed in the chair. "I swear! I'm close to a break through, just give me three more weeks! The baby is due anytime now and he'll be ready to talk." The Commandant, knowing what was going to happen to the baby, thought it over and granted Neil more time. He put the gun away and said, "three weeks and no more. You don't produce, then you and your friends can kiss your asses goodbye." He smirked inwardly as he planned to kill them anyway with or without the information.

At the two o'clock hour, Sam awoke with Neil standing over him as he placed a wet rag on his head. Sam asked, "Where are the others?" Neil answered slowly, "they . . . they slaughtered them all and we might be next." Then Sam asked, "Where did they take you and what did they do?" "They interrogated me again and smacked me around a bit" Neil replied as he massaged his swollen face. Sam sighed and closed his eyes, "I'm so tired of this . . . If they're gonna kill us, then let's get it over with!" Neil replied, "speak for yourself, I want to live and you should too, you've got a baby coming and two women vying for your affection, if that ain't worth living for then I don't know what is." Amidst the surrounding din of gunfire, Sam felt better and reassured in their friendship.

As the days went on and the two men waited for the executioner to come, they spent the time talking about old times and sunnier days. Then on the fifth day of their rebonding, Neil felt he buttered up Sam enough and it was time to get to the truth.

Not wanting Sam to blow his stack like he did the other day, Neil approached the topic by talking about the engagement party and how humiliating it was for him to have been ejected from the festivities. Then he spoke of the day when he went to join the J.U. and they rejected him. Sam felt uneasy about discussing this subject as during their friendship, he kept his participation in the organization and the fact that he was in attendance at the exclusive tribunal that denied Neil's application, a secret. At the time of his rejection, Sam offered words of sympathy to Neil and then the subject was never brought up again, until now. Even though he valued Neil's friendship, there were some aspects about him that disturbed him, although Neil could be funny, witty and a best bud, the creepy side of him left much to be desired. Sam remembered their college days, times when he, Josh and Neil got caught up in drunken barroom brawls, Neil was always the one with the most mouth but when things got too sticky, he was the first one to run. It was his cowardice and crudeness that kept Neil out of JU. Sam said, "If it makes you feel any better, I'm not a member of it either." Knowing he was lying, Neil asked, "why not? You're the infamous Lancealot and that's the sort of cause a hero such as yourself would revel in." "Normally I would've, but I had mixed feelings about it as I wanted to stay with Naomi and raise a family. If I were in the JU, there'd be no way my marriage would have survived and she'd be at home being my dutiful wife while I went gallivanting around defending the defense-less and blowing up things. This doesn't mean that I'm not loyal to the cause, its just not what I want to do." Neil wanted to throttle him for lying so smoothly and tried to keep his rage bottled inside as waiting for Sam to slip up would take more time. Sam maybe a foot soldier and a pawn but it was obvious to Neil that he was a damn good one as no matter how slick the question was presented, Sam's answers were perfectly reasonable and he showed no emotions that even his body language revealed nothing. Neil realized that the only way he could get at Sam now was through Chantel and the snatching of their baby. Neil thought, "If snatching their baby doesn't bring him to his knees, then he's a colder son of bitch than I am."

The day has come and I am in labor. The pain is excruciating but not as painful as delivering a baby by yourself. My captors are outside my cell recording, and they offer no help what so ever as I writhe in pain. After six hours, I am close as this thing inside pushes to get out. I am biting my lip as the pressure on my kidneys and other organs scream for this baby to get off of them and it must have heard my thoughts, as it finally slid out of me tangled in stuff that I had feeling should come later. Even though I know nothing about birthing babies, I knew that something was wrong and I rescued it from out of all that gunk and took the necessary steps to help "Baby Sands" breathe. "Wow, what a great set of lungs!" I thought as it wailed as I cleaned him off with a pillow case and as I wrapped him up in one of the sheets, I suddenly felt glad. Not because my labor was over, but because I was holding a brand new life, one that was produced out of love despite the circumstances.

While basking in my newfound motherhood, they came and took away, (except the food and the sheets covering me) all those comforts I had come to enjoy and exchanged them for Neil and Sam. They were malnourished and dirty, and Sam, being the neat freak that he is, went to the sink to wash as where they were sent, nothing worked. Neil pounced on the food and I tried to save some for Sam but because I was nursing at the time, I was only able to rescue a handful of grapes and two bananas. Neil seized them and Sam smacked him, "we don't steal from women!" I noticed a tenseness between them as Sam gave the stolen fruit back to me, he watched as I nursed his son. I said, "it was for you . . ." He smiled, "you keep it, you need your strength for our baby." When the baby finished, I handed him over to Sam; he hummed a Jewish lullaby and rocked the cranky little one, it burped loudly and then it went to sleep. Sam leaned over and kissed me as he was truly proud. Suddenly, five Rambos burst in and slammed me hard against the rim of the bed; then they snatched the baby out of Sam's arms. He fought valiantly but was stopped by a gun butt to his abdomen and yet, Neil didn't move; he just sat there watching this drama unfold while stuffing his face. We both moaned in pain as our injuries throbbed along with the pain in our hearts as our son was stolen from us. Sam crawled over to me and held me as I sobbed "I didn't even get a chance to name him . . . he was only minutes old!!!!!"

We sat on the floor for hours in each other's arms mourning our son and our insensitive cellmate now lay on the bed where our son was conceived.

The day turned into night and we were still on the floor watching Neil; occasionally, I'd glance at Sam, whose steely brown eyes which usually sparkled with love, now expressed a blazing hatred. I fell asleep but around midnight, was rudely awakened by our captors as they dragged Sam from me. I jumped up to stop them despite one of them putting a gun to my head, I kept fighting, "I'll do anything you want!!! Please don't take him away!!! Take Neil!! Take Neil!!" But they ignored me and left me alone with him.

After they took Sam away, I huddle in the opposite corner of the cell, so I could keep an eye on him. I fear he will harm me in my sleep and now that Sam is gone there is nothing to stop him from doing so. I want to cry but fear my sobs would wake him, so I wish the tears away and think of better days. I am brought back to reality as screams, and gunfire echoes within the building, however, Neil sleeps soundly.

He lay with his back to her and smiled to himself as he sensed her fear. He couldn't wait for the time to reveal to Sam and Chantel the reasons why they were allowed to live so long. It started because he was blacklisted from the J.U, and he wanted to destroy the organization by giving the information about it to the Rambos. At first, his disgrace fueled his reasons for snitching; but when he noticed Sam and Chantel at the metal plant, he decided to kill two birds with one stone. It wasn't until the rebel commander told him that Sam was actually a member of the JU that his jealousy of Sam and his desire for Chantel encouraged him to use them as bargaining chips.

Around 9 a.m., two new Rambo soldiers came to force Neil and Chantel to perform like Chantel and Sam had done since their arrival. Chantel refused and fought them like a feral cat despite triggers being cocked. During the struggle, they wondered where she got the strength to fight considering she had given birth no more than 24 hrs. ago. Tired of their incompetence to settle the woman, it was Neil who subdued her with a stout right cross to the face. The guards laid her upon the bed and haggled over who would do her first, Neil shouted "Back off! Nobody touches her but me!" They trained their guns on him and cocked the triggers. He laughed at them, "Kill me and General Hattib will boil you alive." Fearful of Hatib, they put their guns down and said nothing as they exited the cell.

Unguarded and left alone with Chantel, Neil smiled to himself as his revenge on Sam was now in effect as he prepared to have his way with the one woman who defied him and got away with it. Knowing Sam's deep respect for women and his aversion of harm to them, Neil gained pleasure from the thought of Sam begging him not to defile the woman who captured his heart. Neil recalled their college days when Sam, Josh Baines and he were cruising buddies, Sam earned the nickname "Lance-a-lot" as no matter what the situation, Sam was always the white knight saving all the damsels and becoming friends or lovers with them. Unfortunately for Neil, he usually got Sam's cast offs or the women dated him out of pity or used him to get close to Sam. He dreaded being Sam's squire and tired of trying to convince his peers that he was his own man and didn't need Sam to do anything for him. Now in this place, he felt victorious as he relished the thought of Sam cracking from this torture and telling everything he knew about the Underground in order to save his precious Chantel. Neil was certain that when the Rambos were satisfied with his results, Sam would be killed, Chantel will be his and as an added bonus, he'd be out from under Sam's shadow for good.

While slowly stripping the unconscious woman of the multiple sheets she used as a maternity dress, Neil marveled at her artistry as each layer of material lay perfectly across her body. Feeling like a child unwrapping a Christmas gift; he became light headed after finally reaching her nakedness. Years of wanting sent blood rushing to his head but her vaginal bleeding intimated him and was hesitant; but the more he thought of Sam, winning at everything and making love to her, his determination to destroy him doubled. The thought of winning, intensified his lust and her condition did not matter to him anymore and he fed her with all the force he could muster from his loins. He shouted as he neared climax, "This is for all the women who dumped or used me!" and thrust harder until his seed mingled with her post pregnancy fluids. Although he was physically spent and desparately needing sleep, he suckled her swollen milk laden breasts, and in no time his manhood once again throbbed urgently to life. His thoughts of revenge ebbed and he decided to make love to her as tenderly as he had always fantasized. In his mind, she was awake and enjoying his lovemaking, and worshipping him instead of Sam.

Sam Sands Victorious

In another building where the criminally insane was usually kept before the war, Sam paced like a caged animal in the confines of the padded holding cell. Thoughts of Chantel and his mission at hand occupied his mind and couldn't think of anything else. "I hate this . . . I hate enlisting Chantel into the espionage that I cannot disclose and now I can't protect her from the dangers of this place nor Neil. When I trained with the Underground, they warned us that anyone we involve in this, become expendable. I thought I could handle this but now I am in love with Chantel and I just can't harden my heart! Oh God, why did they take me away this time? What are they doing to her? Why didn't they take Neil away too? I swear if that traitorous dog touches her I'm going to kill him! He deserves to die and Chantel was right; wartime or in peace, no true friend would let any harm come to me or mine. How could he just sit there and watch them take my son away and sleep like nothing happened? God help me, if he touches her . . . he's dead meat . . . ."

It was about noon when the guards came got him to take him back to the other cell. He arrived to see his worst fear come true and there was no guard around enforcing this. Sam's escorts dragged him inside and handcuffed him to the door so he could watch and they laughed at this cruel setup before leaving. "Neil!! Leave her alone!" he screamed as he tried to break free of his bonds, but despite his efforts, Neil ignored him. Time seemed to move slowly and Sam continued to scream until his voice was almost gone, his tears dried up and all he could do was watch. Sam was weak from this emotional torture despite his anger and hatred of Neil welling up inside of him. He was sorry he didn't listen to Chantel and now he was feeling the agony of Neil's revenge.

Two hours later, Neil moaned as his lust finally exhausted; he lay on top of Chantel to rest as he fully drained himself. He kissed her lips and then kissed his way back to her breasts and tasted her milk for the final time. He languished there as he thought of the baby that once suckled from them; but Sam's screams brought him back to his mission at hand. He got up and noticed her blood on himself; he went to the sink and yelled to Sam as he washed, "Damn, that pussy was good! Dude, you've been holding out on me; this is one bitch I wouldn't have minded receiving second hand!" He dressed and went over to him; Sam became more enraged and now wanting to kill his once long time friend. Neil laughed and said, "You don't look so high and mighty now, do you? God, I've been waiting all my life to see you disgraced, and on your knees on the other side of a pity stick!" Sam spit on him, "Spineless son of bitch! You couldn't face me without help, when I get free from these things I'm going to kick your goddamned ass!" Neil laughed as he wiped the spittle off his face, "as you wish, but they know Chantel's identity and about your involvement in J.U. You've been lying to me Sammy boy, all these years, you kept it a secret. But you know, they had some very gruesome tortures planned for her in order for you to spill your guts about the JU.; luckily, I intervened and you should be gratefully kissing my ass cause I'm the reason the two of you are still alive! So buddy boy, if you cherish that little chocolate fantasy of yours and your own ass, then I advise you to talk. Who is the commander of the JU for this quadrant and where is he or she hiding?" Sam spit on him again and said, "None of your fucking business!" Neil's patience was gone, and as all the years of mounting jealousy came to the surface, he howled, "Talk you son of a bitch!" He pummeled Sam until he realized the man was out cold and replied. "Sweet dreams Lancealot, cause this is the last time you'll be able to." Since his efforts to extract information from Sam failed, and his life was on the line, Neil decided to lie his way out of this situation. He called for the guards to take him to the commander and as they came and saw the unconscious man that was chained to the door, they assumed Neil had accomplished his mission and as they escorted him to the command center, he perfected his lies in his head. He reported his fake success to the commander and gave false information of who and where to locate the leader of this region's chapter of the Jewish Underground. He was thanked and as another token of the commander's gratitude, he was granted to witness Sam's and Chantel's demise. Neil didn't want her to die yet, and requested that he be the one to dispose of her. The commander agreed to his conditions and offered him a cigar and a glass of wine to celebrate Neil's victory and told his soldiers to prepare a special feast as an added reward. The commander also told Neil that he could take a shower in his private quarters while he waited for his meal and that a fresh suit of clothing was waiting for him as he was to be freed as per their agreement. Neil smiled as everything was going his way for a change and shook the commander's hand in gratitude.

After Neil finished showering and dressing, Rambo soldiers led him to an empty room where a table with all the finery of a restaurant was laid out for his benefit. Also in the room was a cot for him to sleep if he got tired after his meal. The soldiers stood near the door but allowed Neil to eat in peace. Neil said to himself, "Now this is more like it! This is how freedom tastes!" and he ate and drank heartily.

Meanwhile, the commander gave orders to another set of his soldiers to take Neil back to Sam's cell when he finished; not to witness Sam's death but to remain a prisoner until he saw fit to let him go. The commander laughed aloud, "Mr. Horlbeck is oh so very clever, but not clever enough; he gave us false information but I'm not discouraged, as another source has provided what we wanted to know . . . So I've changed my mind, you can do whatever you wish with Mr. Horlbeck and his friends.

Released from his bonds, Sam awoke on the floor beside the bed where Chantel lay motionless and realized Neil had been removed. He tried to revive her but she didn't move and didn't seem to be breathing well. He ran to the gate and yelled for help. "What wrong?" said one soldier in broken English. Sam pleaded, "Please, take her to the infirmary! She's dying!" The two guards looked through the bars and then the other one shrugged his shoulders, "it happens" they laughed and went back to their post.

It was nightfall when a doctor arrived on the scene. Sam recognized him but neither man made any move that would alert the guards of their friendship. The doctor quickly checked her over and yelled at the guards for allowing her mistreatment; the guards trained their guns on him and he put his hands up in surrender. "Okay okay . . . you win . . . but you must allow me to tend to her in the infirmary or else she'll die. Considering her importance to Commandant Hattib, if she dies, she won't die alone." Fear of Hattib's wrath nor knowing of the new orders, the guards left the men alone as they went to collect medical equipment. Now that they were alone, Sam said, "God knows I'm glad to see you Josh, but how'd you get here and why are you working for them?" Josh said, "I was arrested after curfew and when they found out I was a doctor, they forced me to treat Hattib for salmonella. Enough of my troubles, found out Neil's a snitch and here to pump you about J.U., they're using Chantel at his insistence, as a pawn to get you to crack." "I know; just before you arrived, that cowardly son of a bitch had me chained to the gate of our cell so I could watch him violate her . . . he admitted he was a snitch." The flashback had Sam nearly in tears. "Oh my God; I knew he was a pain in the ass but I never thought he'd do something like this!" said Josh in disgust. "Dammit why didn't I see it coming and how did you know?" asked Sam. Josh replied, "Those Rambo bastards played your friendship with Neil against you, that's why you didn't see it and as far as knowing the mishmash around here, being fluent in Middle Eastern languages helps as I am able to listen in on their discussions and pass it on to JU if able. Yes, I'm a spy too but relax, you and I are still on the same team. Speaking of mishmash, the general gave orders for you, Chantel and Neil to be executed; I came down here to rescue you before those orders were carried out but evidently the order hasn't reached these idiots yet." "Thank God" sighed Sam as he watched Josh finish his examination and then asked, "How is she? Is she going to make it?" Josh's look was grim. "It's a wonder she's held on this long. I gotta work fast if we're going to get out of here before the death squad comes." Suddenly, her heart stopped, he quickly performed CPR, at first it seemed as if it wouldn't work but after his second try she was revived. Then the guards came with the medical equipment and assisted Josh. So engrossed in Chantel, they left the gate open, it would've been a chance to escape, but he didn't want to leave without of the love of his life and mother of his child. They took her out and he followed them to the infirmary and as they took her to the operating room he sat in the waiting room surrounded by his enemy.

During the surgery, Josh and his team worked feverishly to heal the damage caused by the birth and the rape. He wished he had the power to send her away from this hell and cursed Neil for doing this to her and to Sam. Although he had known both men in college, he always felt uneasy around Neil as he seemed so secretive and cold. As his past apprehensions about Neil resurfaced, he felt guilty. "If I had spoken up back in those college days, Sam wouldn't have befriended Neil and this incident would've never happened." He thought this over then decided he had to stop regretting past deeds and concentrate on the task at hand.

Returned to his cell, Sam sat on the bed and questioned whether protecting the Underground was worth all this misery and toyed with the idea of becoming a snitch; but it all changed when a seemingly well rested, well dressed Neil, was tossed into the cell by two new guards. When Neil realized he had been tricked, he pleaded with the guards to take him elsewhere. "You promised I could witness his execution! NO NOOOO!!! Don't leave me in here with him! He'll kill me!!" Sam, so wild with anger and hate, pounced on Neil while the guards were still in the cell with them. They left to give the men room to fight and watched from outside the cell and waited until Neil was an unconscious, bloodied mess before taking him out of there. As they carried him to the infirmary to be patched up, (only to be tortured in other ways later) they laughed as Neil was the joke of the century. Because of his cowardice, they felt he wasn't even worth wasting their time to kill and opted to pass Neil around amongst the prisoners who were hot for a snitch's blood to do the job for them.

A full 72 hour period had passed since Sam beat the crap out of Neil and the finding of a knife from a meal long gone reminded him that he hadn't eaten since then. He sat in a corner and hid the knife under his feet . . . then as if they read his mind, two food bearers came and set meager rations down in the middle of the floor. He didn't move, blink, nor breathe and this prompted them to come closer as they thought he was dead. Quickly, he got that knife from under his feet and stabbed them and broke their necks. After coming down off this euphoria, he got an idea; he took the clothes off the less bloody one and dressed in his clothing, then placed both bodies on the bed and covered them up in a sheet to make it look like two people copulating. He took the keys and rifles then locked the cell; and prayed this plan would work cause he was noticeably shorter and much thinner than his captors.

As he reached other inhabited cellblocks, he revealed his face to let them know he was there to free them. Sam picked out a man in one cell who was built like their captors and dressed him in the Rambos garb. He instructed him to lead them through the halls as if he were a guard taking prisoners to another part of the prison. Along the way, they encountered some guards and they subdued them to gain more costumes. Finally as they neared the entrance, they had amassed a small band of thirty men and twelve women dressed in garb and raided encampments until they were eight hundred strong.

The battle is fierce and many of my fellow rebels are wounded but we fought on and with much of the enemy subdued, we went back for our fallen comrades and got them to safety. After all the fighting in the main prison tower was over, a small band of my fellow rebels and I went back to the infirmary for Chantel and Josh. Neil was there too, but Josh made sure Neil couldn't get at Chantel by duck taping him to a gurney. I wanted to kill him, but Josh had a better idea; and Neil was thrown in a cell filled with captured Rambos. "Traitorous dogs belong with their masters!" I said as Neil pleaded for mercy, but after all these months of torture endured, I did not hear his cries as I had no mercy left.

We got to the prison's administrative building and radioed for assistance from American troops. After sending out our SOS, Josh and I separated as Josh and a small band of our rebels took Chantel and other wounded commrades to the assigned pick up zone, while I along with a few others, searched other parts of the prison for the kidnapped babies. We found them under heavy guard but luck was on our side as other prisoners joined us and we defeated the guards. We took all the children out of there; however, my son was not among them. We captured Commandant Hattib and I interrogated him about my son; he said, "he's sold." I burned with rage; "to who? Speak up or I'll break your fucking neck!" The man scoffed, "I don't know the specifics. We ship them to our country, people there do the rest." I growled like a wild beast and snapped the man's neck anyway. Satisfied to have killed one of the major figures in this war, I said to my comrades, "Victory is ours! Our freedom awaits!" They lauded my speech and began to sing, "America." Feeling uplifted as we ran out of that God forsaken place, we were met with trucks and medvac helicopters in the courtyard, filled with American troops and Red Cross workers, eager to take us to medical facilities miles away. When our army helicopter lifted above the prison, my fellow rebels gave an unified cry of jubilation but I felt empty as despite my acts of heroism, I'm not proud of myself nor am I proud to be a member of the J.U. I'm tired; I'm going to resign my position as I had enough of causing death and destruction and of being betrayed and being the betrayer. I can no longer bare to sacrifice my loved ones and friends for a cause. I won many a battle during my captivity and saved many lives, but nothing matters to me as I can never erase the fact that I jeopardized Chantel's life and failed to save my precious son.

Despite the joy all around him, he could not participate in the jubilation as these ghastly memories swept Sam up in a torrid swell of guilt. All his emotions converged upon his soul at once, allowing his tears to fall and they refused to cease until the helicopter finally touched down thirty minutes later in the safety zone.

As Josh accompanied the group of medtech's wheeling Chantel from the heliport into the rooftop entrance medical facility, Sam came running up to meet them and held her hand as they made their way inside. He continued to walk along side her until Josh stopped him and led him into a waiting area. Josh had that same grim look on his face he had when he first examined her in that cell and trying to stifle a sob, he semi-whispered, "Sam, she needs more surgery . . . ." "What do you mean more surgery? You said she was going to be ok!!" Sam was frantic and began to pace back and forth. Josh said as calmly as he could, "Sam . . . there was way too much damage for me to handle and I did the best I could with the limited equipment in that infirmary . . . . she . . . she needs a hysterectomy and without it we could lose her altogether." Tears welled in both men's eyes, Sam said, "Oh God no, she just changed her stance on motherhood . . . . and I . . . I wanted another chance to be a father . . ." Josh sniffed back his tears as he realized for the first time that Sam was deeply in love with Chantel. Seeing how blinded his friend was by this love and hoping to be the voice of reason, he replied gently, "But Sam . . . you still can be; remember, you're still married to Naomi." Sam looked as if he were struck by lightning as he realized he hadn't thought of Naomi as his wife in a very long time. Yes in the beginning of his captivity, he worried about her but the truth was that he was no longer her passion as the J.U. replaced him and she was more of a fellow soldier moreso than a wife. What kept them bound together was their marriage license, the wedding rings they wore and memories of wedded bliss that faded once the war began. He was confused now and it all showed on his face. Josh asked, "So what are you going to do?" "I don't know; I just . . . I just . . ." said Sam as suddenly he felt faint. He crumpled in a heap in Josh's arms and Josh called for a gurney. After checking Sam's vital signs, he discovered Sam had a fever; upon deeper inspection, he found open wounds on his right arm with signs of infection along with swelling in the elbow and wrist joints which indicated that they were broken. Josh said, "That's my Lancealot, a hero until the end."

FREE AT LAST

We stayed at this medical center for a month as we recuperated from our wounds and our families could be contacted. I was under strict medical care and Sam had a few broken bones even though he never complained during our entire ordeal. He came to visit me often but on this bright and sunny day, he was sad. He said to me, "It's shame that you and I have to go our separate ways now . . . Naomi and her family and mine are coming here to pick me up sometime today. After all we've been through, I've come to realize just how much you mean to me, we make a great team and I want you to know that I was in denial all those years; I love you and always have." I cried as I've longed to hear those his words but now it was too late and my worst nightmare was now confirmed; he was going to be reunited with his wife, the real Naomi Sands and I am going to be alone. Then he told me the truth about his involvement in the Jewish Underground and that the reason why we were allowed to remain alive, was because Naomi was a very high ranking officer and the enemy had a bounty on her. He admitted that he did what a soldier was trained to do and apologized for the charade but I wasn't mad. The truth set me free and my love for him grew even deeper than before as this war brought us closer together and we shared something precious even though it was taken away. We kissed passionately and longingly until we were interrupted by a nurse who announced that Naomi and company had arrived and were waiting for him in the Reception room. He left but came back minutes later with Naomi and the rest of his clan; they all presented me with flowers and gifts as a thank you for my efforts as "Naomi Chantel Sands". However, I was surprised at this outpouring of gratitude from Naomi's folks who didn't like me upon my first meeting with them and felt that I should have never been in attendance at Sam's engagement party or wedding. They seem like changed people now and even hugged me as if I were family. As we talked and my spirits lifted some, the realization that I was right back where I started from, back to being a second fiddle in Sam's life, crept upon me like a ghost and destroyed my happy feelings. I can't wait for these people to leave, that way no one would be able to see me cry.

Six months later, the war was over and as the country began to rebuild, the President awarded Chantel, Sam, Josh and others, congressional medals of honor for bravery during a big ceremony in the newly rebuilt White House. After the awards dinner, the honorees sat at the table with the President and his family as they enjoyed the rest of the evening. Sam kept making eye contact with Chantel despite the fact his wife was sitting next to him. This was a black tie affair and he kept looking Chantel up and down, noticing every inch of her curves as the material of her gown laid gently across them and she kept thinking of how sexy his body was underneath that expensive tuxedo. Chantel nearly exploded when he asked her to dance but quickly recovered and let him lead her there. They slow dragged and he slyly grinded into her. She said enjoying it, "Don't you think you should back up some? Everyone is watching us, including your wife." He replied, "I don't care; I can't help how I feel." Despite herself, she said, "Sorry Sam, I can't do this, I can't be your chocolate fantasy anymore." "please . . . don't deny me . . . I love you . . . I'm going to divorce Naomi so I can do what's right for us." "That's just it Sam, it's not right. What you loved was a combination of two women you created back in that cell. You'll never be satisfied with one part of me and one part of Naomi." With everyone watching, he kissed her with that same passion he gave her back in the prison, then he walked away. She was stunned, and so was everyone else, including the President Of the United States. As reporters ran after Sam, some surrounded Chantel and she refused to comment and then the President came over to ask what happened. Still in shock, she cried "I don't know!" as the President put his arms around her. As he and three of his Secret Service agents steered her away from the leering crowd, they passed Naomi's table and her face was full of rage. But her attention was soon diverted by cameramen and reporters trying to get her side of the story.

2 YEARS LATER

Never will I ever take freedom for granted as it has been 2 years since the war ended and life is good! The United States is rapidly healing from the scars that the insane war left and things for me are getting back to normal. Because my ordeal in, and out of the war was so well publicized, I have a new job as an ambassador representing the President's new United People Program. I can't believe it, but I'm a high ranking public figure now; not bad for a little black girl from the projects! This job is rewarding as it makes me feel good that I'm helping cultures and races across our nation to bond and to embrace freedom as a whole. I am kept so busy that my personal needs have been put on hold. Sure I enjoy life's pleasures, but one of those pleasures includes Sam and I try very hard not to think of him. It's just too painful . . . .

"Ahhh . . . . its Saturday and I have nothing planned and I like it. Peace and quiet that's what I need; time for some "me" time. I think I'll hit the hot tub and take a long soak and later maybe take a drive; yeah that's a plan!" thought Chantel as she prepared for her activities. After getting all her essentials set up for the hot tub, the door bell rang. "Who the hell could this be? I'm not expecting anybody." She put on her robe and went to open the door; she was shocked to see Naomi standing at her doorstep. "What are you doing here?" "visiting you obviously." Naomi said as she entered without being invited. "So this is how political puppets live . . . very impressive . . ." "what's that supposed to mean?" "Thanks to your little stunt at the Presidential Awards dinner, you robbed Sam of everything he's worked hard for." Naomi said sarcastically. "I did no such thing . . . look, I don't have time for this; state what's on your mind and get out." retorted Chantel. Naomi sighed, "Fine, I'll be brief . . . even though you stole my husband from me, I'm here on his behalf. He's been depressed over the loss of his son and hoped to find some peace by being with you but your rejection pushed him over the edge. Now he lies in the hospital with pneumonia and has given up; he wants to die. . Chantel, despite what's happened between the three of us, I still care about him and I'm not ready to bury him, and I don't think you are either, so please, I'm urging you to go to him." Chantel replied, "I'll think about it." Naomi said as she handed her a piece of paper with information about the hospital, "Don't take too long thinking about it." and then she left.

She recalled how Sam's behavior at the awards dinner brought about the scandal that was broadcast nationwide. *"National War Heroes Caught in Love Tryst!" "Truth Revealed at Presidential Awards Ceremony, President Shocked!"* Hawked the bylines of newspapers days after and the worst insult came from the supermarket tabloids as they boasted a pictures of Chantel and the President as he had consoled her and the by lines read, *"President and War Heroine Lovers?" "Chilvary Is Not Dead! President Protects War Heroine From Angry Ex Lover"* The shit hit the fan for everyone involved as their reputations were scrutinized by the media and the war weary public. Despite the unnecessary hoopla over the situation, she felt guilty that the public related more to her than Sam. Their ordeal was trivialized as a tragic love story and somehow the public made Sam out to be a backstabbing villain as he used Chantel to masquerade as his wife and the regional leader of the Jewish Underground.

Chantel tried hard to let the world know it was Sam's heroism and quick wit that kept them alive and brought them home safely, but her efforts failed as it seemed America needed a scapegoat to divert from the serious impact the war made on its shores. And because of this, Sam's world fell apart as he lost his job, Naomi divorced him and he was shunned. Two weeks after the incident happened, she tried to help Sam rebuild his life, but she lost contact with him as he suddenly disappeared. He had gone so deep underground that even the Secret Service, the FBI nor America's best detectives could find him. Her efforts extended for months afterwards until she realized, it was best to let him come to her as she spent too much of her new found affluence on Sam and not the job the President selected her to do. After mulling these things over, she was too upset now and soaking the hot tub was not so important; all she could see was Sam in a hospital suffering because of her.

The next day, Chantel went to the hospital to see Sam. She was shocked to see him looking so helpless as he was hooked up to so many machines. His once robust body was now a pale and thin form that slept soundly as heavy doses of medications pumped intravenously through his veins. Even though she did not want to disturb his rest, she could not resist kissing his forehead and whispered, "Oh Sam, I . . . I'm so sorry. I never meant for this to happen . . ." Tears slowly eased down her cheeks as she was truly remorseful of how things turned out between them as her fantasy had come true and she almost lost him. Just then, his eyes fluttered opened and with a raspy voice gave a weak "hello". She kissed his hand, "I love you Samuel Sands and always have . . ." He wiped away her tears, "You know . . . during our imprisonment, I realized I was in denial for such a long time about my feelings for you . . . and now I'm damn sure I want to marry you and be with you, forever." More tears rolled down her face as she consented. "but you have to get well first." "Now that you're here, I feel better already . . . ."

Three weeks later, Sam was being discharged from the hospital and he was overjoyed that Chantel agreed to be his wife. He waited for her to pick him up and take him back to her place to stay as Naomi had won the house in the divorce settlement and because of the scandal he wasn't able to find a decent place to live. His heart beat wildly at the thought of being married to her as she had been his chocolate fantasy ever since they met 12 years ago and as he sat waiting for her, he recalled that night of their first meeting vividly.

He and Josh were leaving their favorite restaurant when they spotted a couple in the parking lot, shouting at one another and once the woman walked away, everything calmed and the guys figured the spat was over and continued to head for their own car. But suddenly screams were heard, and Sam and Josh ran back toward the couple to see the man holding the woman from behind and wielding a knife to her throat.

Without hesitation, Sam leapt into action and confronted him; the man said, "This ain't none of your business white boy; you don't wanna get cut, so you better move on!" Sam replied, "Then I guess, you'll have to cut me . . ." The man threw Chantel aside and lunged for Sam, but he was ready for the man and hit him below the belt bringing him down like a newly sawed tree. While the man lay on the ground writhing in pain, Sam took his belt and tie off to restrain him and went to attend to Chantel who was shaken from this ordeal. Meanwhile, Josh had gone and got a cop and when he arrived on the scene, he saw that Sam truly had everything under control and as always like all the white knights of history, Sam was victorious and got the girl in the end. Josh shook his head and smiled approvingly, "Lancealot does it again."

Sam and Chantel remained close friends and secretly, for a long time, neither dared to tell that they were each other's fantasy. However, the same year he had met Naomi, Chantel confessed how she felt about him, but by then it was too late because he was already smitten by the other woman. It wasn't until they were captured during the war, that the truth came out. Sam tried to be faithful to Naomi and didn't want to admit it at first, but when their captors forced him to make love to Chantel, he used those moments to unleash his true passions for her and he was sure she could tell. It wasn't until the birth of their son in that hellhole, that it all was confirmed and now all their fantasies are now true as they would be soon walking down the aisle in matrimony to become Mr. Samuel and Mrs. Chantel Jones-Sands.

Finally, she arrived and as he watched her approach, the graceful swaying of her curviness and slight bounce of her bountiful breasts made urgent needs apparent and he knew that once they got home, he was going to make up for lost time and give her his passion without any coaxing or restraint.

NEIL

FROM ONE PRISON TO ANOTHER

In a federal prison in Washington D.C., Neil Horlbeck is serving twenty years for treason against America and ten years for rape and abuse of Chantel. As he watches the evening news, the big story is about Sam and Chantel's wedding. It captured all the news hawks attention only because the President of the United States stood in for Chantel's father and led her down the aisle. As the camera zoomed in on Chantel and the President, Neil felt an erection blooming as the wedding dress she wore accentuated her curvy body and the thought of having her again flashed in his mind. He smiled to himself proudly as what he did to her in that cell during the war was his crowning achievement; he couldn't believe the stamina he had then to continue the sex act for so many hours. With that memory, he began to masturbate; "when I get out of here, I'm coming for you baby. And this time, you'll be awake so you can feel my every touch!" He closed his eyes and pretended she was there with him; he envisioned himself suckling at her breast tasting her milk again then thrusting himself deep inside her. The thought of being inside her and hearing her cries of ecstasy, caused his manhood to throb and in minutes he violently erupted. He vowed, "when I get out, there's going to be a repeat performance and when I'm done with you . . . you'll yearn only for me and ol' Sammy boy won't be there to stop me!!" He relished that thought too as it was his plan to torture Sam like the Rambos did to him and then while his life long buddy begged for mercy, he'd oblige him by snuffing his life out like a cigarette. He laughed and exclaimed loudly, "It's gonna be so fucking sweet!!!"

CHAPTER 3

AN EXCERPT FROM KIMBALL STREET

WHAT'S SO SPECIAL ABOUT KIMBALL STREET?

Let me count the ways . . . .

It's the only street where New Year's celebrations are held under kitchen tables just so bullets won't find a target . . . .

One is considered an outcast because he/she doesn't do drugs, or alcohol and has a job . . .

You say Hello/ speak out of courtesy they stare at you . . .
        You don't speak,
they still stare but they want to beat you up now because you didn't speak . . .

There's a crowd sitting on and around the stoop of a nice looking house, however, they don't live there or even know the person who does . . . .

People fight over parking spaces that don't belong to them.

Block parties aren't for the people who live on the block.

Abandoned buildings make great wild life habitats

Welcome to . . . Kimball Street!

An Excerpt From Kimball Street

Oh I, Oh I yeah Oh I, Oh I yeah
An Excerpt from Kimball street,
An Excerpt from Kimball street

I got a story just for you;
told from a victim's point of view
sickNtired taking guff from you,
gonna fight back that's what I'll do

Liquor house, selling drugs,
stealing just for fun,
look out boys here they come, drive by shooters
with their big big guns

Disrespect, blight and neglect
spreading across the nation
Sick patterns set for future generations!

Vandalize me scandalize me
shoot me with your gun,
but with God as my shield and my guide, you ain't got
enough to make me run from Kimball,
Off Kimball Street—where?
Off Kimball, From Kimball street
An excerpt from Kimball Street

THIS WAY OF LIVIN

Sleepin', eatin' and livin' politicians lies.
Seein', smellin' tastin' poverty and listenin'
to unwanted babies cries

Mad dogs and rabid vermin greetin' you
in the littered streets,
rapists, muggers, awaiting in the dark
for you to meet.

Sons of worried mothers, uncarin' and so
damned carefree.
Sadness and evil is takin' over all human life.
This way of livin' isn't what I want it to be,
and I swear I'll get out of here before it overtakes me.

I Believe I Can Fly-
Exhaled Housewife
VERSION

I believe I can fly
Barney was arrested by the FBI
that was news of yesterday,
I'm a housewife with much to say

I believe I can fly
I believe I can fly, I believe I can touch the sky!
Tired of being married to the same old guy
all he does is make me cry; I believe I can fly.

I believe I can soar, kicked his sorry ass out my door;
he refused to pay child support
he got locked up by the court

I believe I can fly
Cause his ass got thirty days,
gonna party a thousand ways

I believe I can fly
Don't know how but I'm gonna try
spread my wings and fly away
all I need is a hunky date
I believe I can fly

I believe I can soar,
just come in my open door,
But don't get too comfy right away
cause this housewife wants to play,
I believe I can fly!!!!!

RESPECT IN THE NEW MILLENNIUM

A LETTER TO THOSE THAT RAISED ME

To My Mother and All the Adults That Raised Me:

Mom, back then during my adolescence, I couldn't see how I would benefit from the reasons why we went to bed so early, why we had to play in the front of our house and when we were able to leave, still could not go far and had to be in the house by 9 p.m. Or why you had to be tougher on us girls when it came to chores and how we carried ourselves, or why we were the only kids in our little circle of friends who had jobs to help pay rent and bills. But as you've helped me grow up to travel down life's delicate winding road, I've found that those lessons that were taught and against which, I sometimes rebelled, are becoming handy now that I am an adult with a family of my own.

But tonight, as I write this while sitting on my stoop, in a quiet protest of my neighbors disrespect, dislike of me, and the abuse of my property, something odd has embraced me as snatches of respect lessons replay in my mind. I can never forget growing up in the 2000 block of Christian Street where life was like living in a village. I had more parents and guardians without ever knowing the displeasure of foster care or having social services labeling our family as dysfunctional. Sure, we weren't perfect and were just as poor as everyone else, but the negative influences that had befallen other families had not touched us. I cannot speak for my siblings, but I personally was too scared of the wrath of you and "the village" to give in to those negative influences! However, my deja vu is caused by the memory of our neighbor Mrs. Jackson. I remember how mean she was and had an extreme dislike of kids.

She didn't like the noise or the mess that was usually left on her sidewalk by kids that had the freedom to roam as they pleased. I remember being eight or nine, and being not allowed to leave the front of the house! I didn't like this ruling, but it kept us out of trouble and taught us to respect other people and their homes. Mrs. Jackson had her own way of disciplining the offenders; if a kid was caught sitting, standing or whatever on her property, she would dump from a second floor window a bucket of urine on them! I thought the woman was crazy! But thought it funny when it happened to a childhood friend who broke the "Don't bother the old folks rule" on a dare. We called him, "Mr. Piss Pot" until were almost grown! Remember those years before Mrs. Jackson died and how she took a shine to us? She was always asking could we go to the store for her or for us to help around her house and unbeknownst to you, she paid us well and occasionally, brought us treats whether we worked or not.

But despite the niceness to us, she was still mean to the others and I guess she took pity on us because we were the last of the "good" kids on the block. I came to realize that she wasn't born mean, but became a lonely soul after the death of her husband. They had no children of their own but I remember Mr. Jackson always having something nice to say to us "kittens" as he used to call us. I really didn't know of Mrs. Jackson until he passed away and I assumed that being with her husband kept her happy and the world outside didn't exist as long as they were together. The "Emptying of the Piss Pot" was probably provoked by her self made isolation, having no idea of what children were about, and having to endure the cruelties from the neighborhood kids. So here I am decades later, sitting on my stoop on the 2000 block of Kimball, dealing with a new breed of offenders and sympathizing with Mrs. Jackson's plight. Whereas Mrs. Jackson was hassled by unruly children, I have problems with trespassing children and adults, with their drugs and alcohol, dog mess & breeding, mingled with disrespect that makes me want to piss on them too! However, I did do a variation of the "Piss Pot" as a second and third generation of a drug family was sitting on my stoop and railing. Despite signs on the glass panes of my front door that scream, "DO NOT SIT ON RAILING OR STEPS", there was at least ten kids using my home as their personal playground. I kindly asked then to move and the older ones cursed at me and the younger ones mimicked them. So while they were all having a laugh at my expense, I went upstairs to my bathroom to prepare my version of the "Piss Pot", which is a combination of warm water and baby shampoo. The color of the shampoo made it look like urine and was supposed to be a no tears formula; unfortunately, I brought a generic brand which made my harmless concoction an eye irritant. Normally I am the voice of reason, but like Mrs. Jackson, they pushed my buttons and I joyously dumped it on them from my second floor window!

Well, when I left home and got married and started my family here on Kimball Street. I didn't know the people here had so many problems nor did I know that their problems would affect me too. As you and all the others from our Christian Street village have taught all the aspects of respects, I find that Kimball St., keeps demanding it but never offers it in exchange. I've been here over a decade and I keep hoping things will change. I would move but this would only boost the egos of my annoying neighbors as they would take pride in thought of chasing me off the block, and, who is to say, that no matter where I go, the same problems won't exist? (I'd rather not jump out of the frying pan only to jump into the fire, to coin a phrase.)

I often listen to the ramblings of the so called parents of the children of the block as you can't help but listen as they purposely broadcast it loudly enough for everyone to hear. But their lecture is totally bullshit as they talk often of how they deserve respect and demand it. The biggest lie I've overheard, was that their kids were raised to respect their home, themselves and others. But if that were true, they'd stay on their own property to make noise, drink beer or smoke crack or pot. They wouldn't trash the block, if they had respect for it and as for themselves, they wouldn't refer to one another as motherfuckers or bitches. (Their words, not mine). Kimball Street has made me realize just how valuable those lessons on respect really were. I'm teaching my daughter these same lessons, but its a hard thing to do as even though this street is in desperate need of respect, it doesn't recognize it when it is applied through me or her. I can only assume, some of the Kimball St. residents' ideas of respect clash with mine.

Mom, I know you used to say, that I didn't have to like a person to respect them. They don't like nor respect me and what's mine and yet, I still try to set an example despite not liking what's going on. Despite my efforts, I have to admit, Kimball Street is slowly eroding all the respect I used to have for it.

And to that village that raised me, I owe you a lifetime of gratitude! You taught me that whatever I do is a reflection on my family and by association, you too! Case in point, I remember my youngest brother's Godmother, Ms. Vi. She was in her eighties and needed the help of a cane to walk, but despite her disabilities, she packed a mean left hook! During my teen years, I was "rebellious" only when I was away from Christian Street and its watchful eyes. One day, my other brother and I, were on our way to school and as we rode the bus to get to our North Philly destination, we sat in the back of the bus with our fellow traveling pals. I recall us laughing aloud and cursing right along with our friends; but at that time though, the worse cuss words for us were damn, shit and hell, I said the word damn real loud in response to something deep one of my friends said. Next thing I know, Ms. Vi came out of nowhere and beat me and my brother with that cane. Not only did she punish us on that bus, but she told on us and when we got home, we got the ass whuppin' of a lifetime by mom. Our crime? Disrespect of ourselves and everyone else by exhibiting rowdy and distasteful behavior on that bus. Nowadays, its the norm and stronger words are used and the behaviors of some of the people today are much more disrespectful and uncouth. For instance, pot smokers usually sneak tokes in the back of the bus, or in a darkened movie theater and (I gotta chuckle here), and think no one will smell it, the smell won't bother anyone and they won't get caught! The same applies to smokers in public places, as they don't see this as being disrespectful to others but believe its their constitutional right to have love, life, liberty and the pursuit of happiness by doing rude things! Most incidents like these are ignored because of the "new Laws" of confrontation; in other words, one can no longer ask a smoker of any kind to put out the butt, without getting a serious foot in the butt! The same goes for people with loud walkmans or just people with bad attitudes in general. Ms. Vi must be up in Heaven shaking her head in disgust at the way people behave today, as it seems everything previously taught to us by our "villages" and parents are becoming extinct. As I sit here and reflect, I feel so confused. I could really use some of that Mom/Village wisdom and back up systems of those bygone days of my youth. Even though your teachings have gotten me this far in life, I'm beginning to feel that I am the only one who values and still maintains what I've been taught.

Is the "Kimball Street" mentality the norm for this new millennium? Could it be that I'm stuck in a time warp and the world's values changed while I was in a Rip van Winkle-like sleep? Or could it be, my life and its adventures have been nothing but dreams of the future, by a little kid with a lot to learn?

Sigh I don't think there's answers for these questions but despite all this confusion, and if I hadn't said so in the previous paragraphs, I want you to know, I am grateful and blessed to have had you all guide me and you did a great job in my upbringing. Well I am going in now as its really late and the mosquitoes are biting hard. I'll write to you again soon,

Lovingly and respectfully,

Your daughter

WHEN IN ROME . . .

In 1985, I took a job as a mail clerk for a small travel agency, in which unbeknownst to me at the time of my hiring, I was the token black. The majority of the staff were Italian American and its owners offered an "orientation trip" to all employees with a choice to go to Italy, England or Spain. Of course, I chose England because I didn't know any foreign languages and England has black communities. However, by majority vote, Spain and England were ruled out and that Thanksgiving weekend of 1985, I was on my first plane ride ever and my destination was Italy.

On the bus to JFK airport in New York, the others sat in back of the bus while I sat alone in the front; the statement made was, "we don't have to associate with you outside the office." Like water off a ducks back, I let it slide and made friends with our Sicilian bus driver. At the airport, I discovered my ticket was for first class which meant I was sitting with upper management while the others were in economy class. It had occurred to me that this gesture was done out of fear of being reported to the NAACP or being slapped with an Affirmative Action lawsuit. I mulled these facts over but I decided to enjoy the free ride as far as it could take me and I had no intentions of staying employed there anyway.

Arrival in Rome was interesting as I thought I was being molested by a pervert as someone kept pinching my ass! By the time I reached customs, I was ready to kill the bastard! The South Philly came out in me and I loudly accused my traveling companions. This caught the attention of the Gendames (cops with capes and white gloves!) My boss told me to quiet down or I was going to jail and the company was not going to bail me out and that pinching of the ass was a friendly gesture of admiration. So, I endured the pinching at our late arrival of the audience with the Pope, all over Rome, in Pompeii, Bologna, Florence, Sorrento, and on the beautiful and romantic Island of Capri.

Not only did I discover the meaning of an ass pinch, I discovered that in this day and age that there are still some people over there who have never seen a black person before! When we were getting on the launch in Naples to take us to the Island of Capri, a small truck was coming off the launch onto the pier; however, the driver looked directly at me and then crashed his truck into a post! Every head turned and looked at me as if it were my fault! When I looked at all those glaring eyes that burned all around me, I understood that the man saw my lone black face in a sea of white ones. One of my co workers made a joke out of it and said they should charge a $25 admission just to see or touch my skin. Again I let it slide. Despite all the racial slurs and other misconduct of my fellow companions, I did make friends with an Austrian tour guide who felt my pain of isolation. She told me that my traveling companions were idiots as they would kill to get a tan as nice as my coloring and that I should hold my head up proudly because I was the envy and the admiration of the people who pinched me although they remained anonymous.

Thanks to my Austrian friend, I hung out with some of the native Italians and the trip wasn't so bad after that. I have more Italian adventures but I shall save them for another time, but whenever you get a chance to go to Italy, see all that you can see and when in Rome, do as the Romans do; eat when they eat, drink when they drink, and pinch back and wear padding just in case you are "envogue" or have a really great ass!

A Wicked Turn

It began just like any normal school day until something strange happened in Ms. Clark's class. We students were riled up over the fact that we were just mere days from the Christmas holiday and looked forward to all of the food and holiday loot we would get . . . however, we forgot that we weren't dismissed from school yet and most of us from Kindergarten to grade eight behaved in manners that would make the strictest of discipliners pull their hair out in clumps.

Boy, were we bad! We were told that we'd get a lump of coal for Christmas once Santa Claus caught wind of our misbehavior. Of course, none of us believe that baloney and what not, because we know that our parents have already bought our gifts and not wanting to be labeled as "bad parents" they'll give them to us anyway! Let the fun begin I say! However, in my class, something happened to Ms. Clark as her sweet and funny manner disappeared and she began to growl and hiss at us like the other teachers do. And then, when we thought she would blow the final gasket, she just smiled. We didn't know what to make of this until the smartest kid in our fifth grade class, Johnny B.; decided to make us laugh by making farting sounds under his armpits.

We laughed but tension filled the air when Ms. Clark told him she was sending a note to his parents and he said out of nowhere, "So, I don't care!" She smiled as a strange look was in her eyes and she kinda muttered, "SO be it!" and went back to her desk. We all laughed and thought the whole exchange was funny until every time Johnny B. the smartest kid in the class spoke, he said, "I don't care!"

We thought he was pulling a fast one on us and of course we laughed but stopped when the Principal came in our room to give

Johnny the Student of the Month award for the third month in a row. The Principal said to Johnny B., "what an achievement! You're the only student to earn this award three months in a row! Congratulations Johnny!" Poor Johnny; although he beamed with pride and gratitude, he was having a tough time trying to keep his mouth clamped shut, but the words came out loud and clear: "SO! I DON'T CARE!" Now, that scared us as you know what that meant; in the Principal's eyes it was a big dose of disrespect and we could see that he thought Johnny B. had gone nuts. He hauled Johnny into his office and when he came out, he was sent home with a note to his parents requesting that Johnny see a doctor. Goodbye Johnny B., we're gonna miss you. And Ms. Clark's smile seemed to say, "one down and twenty-nine more to go."

We were confused momentarily but then like an unseen phantom or some silly gas drifting upon us, our class's mood shifted and we began to act up again. Then Susan K, aka the Gabber, talked and talked and ignored Ms. Clark while she was giving us instructions on how to do the math problems on the board. She smiled in Susan's direction and muttered, "see no evil, hear no evil."

Suddenly, Susan began to fade in and out like a ghost and we couldn't hear her very well. I could see (in between fade ins) how really upset she was as ghostly tears streaked down her cheeks. No one could hear her sobs and some kids ignored her completely. Ms. Clark went on with her lesson as if nothing was wrong and her smile was one of satisfaction and seemed to say, "Twenty-eight to go!" We were really spooked now as seeing Susan fade in and out like that could only happen in a ghost story and we began to suspect our dear Ms. Clark was a real life witch.

During recess, we talked about what happened in Ms. Clark's because we were too shook up to play. A group of us decided that we'd tell the Principal, but we changed our minds as he'd probably send us home with notes to our parents that saying we need to see a doctor too and nobody wanted that. So after recess, we were very good and tried our bestest not to upset Ms. Clark.

Then something strange happened, the class was so quiet that you could hear a pin drop! And soon other teachers and the Principal came in to tell us how proud they were of us and they never did that before! It was then that I realized that we students weren't just riled during the holiday season, we were riled up all the time! The strange things began because Ms. Clark was tired of taking our guff. Well, I tell you, I saw her and all the teachers in a new light and I promise to behave from now on as I don't want to be doomed to a life of saying, "So! I don't care, nor do I wish to be turned into mist. And mostly, I want the happy, nice, and treat giving Ms. Clark back again.

By the end of the day, Susan was back to normal but she didn't talk so much and Johnny B. came back with his parents but the "So I don't care" attitude was gone. Everything was good again and as Ms. Clark dismissed us, I was curious to know and asked all my questions at once. "Ms. Clark, we aren't that bad, are we? How did you do those things and are you a witch?" Her (harmless) sweet smile was back and she said, "yes dear you children are that horrible and to answer your other questions . . ." (her eyes turned cat-like and glowed) "that's for me to know and you to find out!"

Gulp That was good enough for me!

WEREWOLVES IN WEST PHILLY

I am enjoying this lovely winter evening as I await the bus to take me to my cozy little home in South Philly. I just left my doctor's office, here in West Philly and she gave me a clean bill of health. Good news does make one feel better as a person such as myself should not have so many symptoms that could be a part of any number of diseases.

Well anyway, the bus arrived and I paid my fare and received my bus transfer graciously as I beamed with happiness over my good news. I must have been too happy as I unknowingly got off the wrong stop for the transferring bus I need. Being unfamiliar of the area, I reached out in desperation to a Hindi woman and asked if she could tell me where to catch the bus to South Philly. She replied, "No." Then I asked her about the bus to Center City and she said as she walked away, "No speaka English." Minutes later, a well dressed gentleman approached and I asked him the same questions. He seemed friendly and he told me where the stop was and that he'd escort me as it was his destination too. While walking, he struck up a conversation full of caution and mentioned how dangerous the area was and that I should never walk the streets of West Philly alone. After he described the dangers to watch out for, the last offense on the list made me laugh hard as he said that I should beware of the Werewolves. I laughed so much that I didn't realize he was leading me to an abandoned lot. I was in serious danger but I continued to laugh cause his story was stupid. He pushed me down and I stopped laughing. He planned to harm me but as he laughed at his triumph of getting over with such a silly line, I decided to let this perp know who's the boss and enlighten him with the truth about werewolves.

The truth is, there are no werewolves in West Philly because they like a much more dangerous climate and reside in Camden, New Jersey. And Vamps or vampires such as myself, live in South Philly . . . He began to tremble and pissed in his pants as I rattled off more truths about "us" mythical creatures than he could stand. I smiled at this human's blissful ignorance and he screamed as my fangs flashed in the light of the moon that now shone and I came to the conclusion that my visit to the doctor was a waste of time because I wasn't sick, I was just hungry.

After finishing off my griot friend, I decided I didn't need the bus either and flew home instead. While in flight, feeling the winter air filter in and out of my batwings, I proved several theories; a good night flight does the body good, honesty is the best policy and fear is the best tenderizer for the meat of prey!

ROSES & BEAUTY

The world isn't all roses and beauty,
there is darkness and evil too,
but the decision of which way to go,
is totally up to you!

Oh I how I wish to see more roses,
and the nature of the sweetest bloom,
unfortunately my darling,
we live in a new millennium
that only harks of victims and gloom.

But as I said before,
the decision of which way to go
is totally up to you

And if there is,
only the tiniest fraction of love
Be rest assured that hope will come to clarify
any disillusioned view.

ROMANTIC BLISS

May our words merge into a melodic phrase,
ending not with a period,
exclamation point,
or question mark
but yields a gentle touch,
that yields unto a kiss and builds into a story
that transforms life into such romantic bliss.

KIMBALL ST

K is for the kinship that this street lacks

I is for the insults one must allow to roll off one's back

M is for the misery that comes from the rejection of change

B is for the bullshit that often turns into rage

A is for the Almighty who keeps us sane

L is for the lascivious ones that roam free

L is for the love that is gone and lost on Kimball Street.

S

T.

PLEA

(it was either this or panhandle on the streets)

Children of mine
with bellies that need feed
And needed shoes for rapidly
growing feet

Continuous bad days
No money to live or spend
Stumbling blocks of low paying job
When's the darkness gonna end?

Walking miles to work because I missed the bus
Sucking on a borrowed cough drop
because I can't afford lunch

No friends around
Body's breaking down
I'm in life's cesspool
I can't swim and I'm gonna drown

Would you be so kind?
I'm in a bind
And treat me gently
'cause I'm losing my mind

How I wish to escape
this life's every scrape
To sit and enjoy a beach
where troubles can't go
and bill collectors can't reach

SIGH . . . *welcome to my life* . . .
If you can sympathize with these words
and you want to wish me luck
I encourage you to buy this exciting book
Because I desperately need the bucks!!